RHYTHM ROGER

RHYTHM ROGER

The Secrets Of Electon

HIMANSHU RAI

Published by
Invincible Publishers

Published by
Invincible Publishers
201A, SAS Tower, Sector 38, Gurugram 122003
Phone: +91-124-4034247, +91 9355675555
www.i-publish.in

First Published in 2020

ISBN: 978-93-89600-57-5

Printed by: Excel Printers Pvt. Ltd.

Success is nothing without your appreciating smiles.
Miss you, Papa and Mummy.

Contents

Acknowledgment

Thank you Sona, my dear wife, for always being by my side and supporting me in my work. It would not have been possible without you and your critic views, which helped me to frame my every story.

This story carries your name, Rhythm, my dear son, and I am proud and thankful to you for your brilliant questions you asked while you listened to this story and helped me add lines and content which could make this story more engaging and exciting.

Thanks to my family members for always having been there for me as a support pillar and for appreciating my work. You praised, guided, and helped me to reach where I am today.

Thanks to my friends and colleagues who always buy a copy of my book on just a single call. Thanks for your love and support.

Thanks to all my readers, blogger reviewers, and followers for reading my books and appreciating them. It's your feedback and suggestions which motivated me more to write better. Every comment from you matters a lot to me. Every single word that you say about my book helps me to frame my next story and correct my mistakes. Please keep sharing your feedback. Thanks again.

If I have missed someone, do forgive me, as you all are my family, and I am thankful to each one of you.

Preface

What will you prefer between the two mentioned below:

1. Football or Smartphones?
2. Basketball or Smartphones?
3. Hide n Seek or Tablet?
4. Running around trees or Pub G?
5. Hugging or scrolling on a mobile screen?
6. Talking with friends or commenting on Facebook and WhatsApp?

If most of your answers are the second ones, then our planet is in danger. I am not sure if Roger can save our world, but he will not let any stone unturned to protect the future.

Noise of Electon

She was running in a forest full of towering trees which were tall enough to reach above the clouds. It was dark, and she was used to this darkness. The darkness had been all over there for the past twenty years. Anagol was the name of the woman who ruled this electromagnetic world named Electon, for the past ninety-six years. She was gifted to this world as its queen by her father, Edison. Since then, Anagol ruled this dark world and helped the human world to reach new heights of achievements.

Anagol was slim, had purple eyes, wore a black skinny fit dress, and had glazing white lines all over her body. All of her hair was perfectly placed and tied on top of her head. She was born with unique qualities, and those qualities made her the Queen of Electon. She was born with time-varying conditions. This enabled her to change her way and speed as per the other person's movement. She had an extraordinary power using which she could respond to anyone by a change in physical phenomena such as sound, light, temperature, pressure, or position. She had a round black mark at the centre of her forehead by which she could convert any physical variable as per her wish. Her powers lay at the centre of her forehead, which gave her an enigmatic look.

Apart from this, she had a different power – a power to run in a sinusoidal direction and that too, with a speed of more than two hundred kilometres per hour. (In the human world, in mathematical terms, a sinusoidal wave is a smooth periodic oscillation curve which develops a continuous wave. Anagol had powers of sinusoidal waves because of which, it was always a tough task to catch her or shoot her.

That night, she was again running at the same speed because another power was behind her to take her to death. The one who was following her was not someone strange to her, but with time, he had gathered the strength to take over Electon.

She turned around to check on her follower while still running at her maximum speed. She was alarmed and terrified as he was coming after her quickly, travelling via air. By his movement, she understood that he had gained energy since the war ended between them some years back. She tried her power to change the physical phenomena of the follower but he escaped by her fire. She took long steps changing her direction in every millionth second, and then she heard the sound of a red fireball being fired by the follower. She turned again to check and decided to change the physical position of the red fireball but she saw it coming towards her faster than her expectation. She tried to change her position but failed. She was sure that the red fireball would hit her and her baby, whom she was carrying in her arms. Unblinking, she looked at her baby who was wrapped in a silver sheet of the element Vanadium. Anagol knew the follower was not only after her but also intended to remove her baby from Electon to be the ruler. Remembering his intention, she covered her baby with her body as the red fireball hit her on her back. She was pushed with great force and flew in the air to half a kilometre, still holding her baby with all her strength. She bumped into a tall tree and then fell on thorny plants. Even the darkness of Electon was in fear of finding its Queen in that state.

She was close to Mount Spuder and her destination. Mount Spuder was the tallest mountain of Electon with not a single sign of grass on it. It was not spread far in measures of distance but was taller than any peak in the human world. The darkness of Electon grew darker with the fog of clashes. Anagol looked up for help and then turned to check on the follower. She stood back holding her baby and then turned as someone in the smoke of fire could be seen walking towards her for her soul. Anagol was hurt and bleeding. She supported herself with her one hand and pulled herself back to stand. She took a heavy breath to absorb most of the electromagnetic waves into her lungs and then, before he could reach her, she gathered all her power and fired from her black mark, creating a fire that was sufficient to generate lava at that spot. She then looked up and within a millionth second, she flew in the air taking sinusoidal curves to the top of the peak. The man behind the smoke, whose face could not be seen, tried to safeguard himself and jumped on the other side. He then stood in anger and shouted, making a noise which was so loud that many trees in that forest uprooted and fell on the ground. His sound was loud enough to create a quake and shiver in the ground. The clouds thundered hearing his voice; it was known as the sound of fear in Electon. He was frustrated as he could not go on Mount Spuder–the house of Crawler.

Anagol reached the peak above the green clouds and fell outside a cave. Her purple coloured blood had spread all over her body. She was exhausted and injured. In this race to fight and save herself and her child, she lost all her energy and was lying on the ground having been completely drained, still holding her baby.

The peak of Spuder was a place that was not a location to be reached by all. It was covered in the darkness of Electon. Only crawling spiders could be seen all over the place–spiders who were always busy constructing a web, all interlinked to each other, so that information about a prey captured in any network could flow to all spiders. The peak was stinking with a smell of spider larvas and was buzzing with the sound of them crawling. It was said that in Electon, the web of Spuder was so strong that it could even carry information from the human world.

As Anagol was lying at the peak, her body disrupted the web network, informing all the spiders of the prey. The smell of her blood was sufficient to attract them and so thousands of spiders started rushing to her. One spider would take only seconds to eat her completely, and thus, were jumping and running to reach her. She was unconscious. She was not moving. The peak was disturbed by her visit and by the sound of her son's wails. Hungry spiders with shining white eyes were turning out from all over the place. They were jumping over the rocks and sliding over the old dark tree, kicking each other with their tenth leg and rushing to have at least some part of the prey. Few were about to reach her and snatch her body parts in their hunger when suddenly, a loud sound of crawling was heard. The sound was epic on its own. Hearing that sound, all the small spiders turned to run away, leaving Anagol in her state. They started making a typical sound of fear and respect, hiding behind rocks and stones. Grey clouds started gathering over the cave as if they were welcoming the master of Spuder.

From the darkness of the cave appeared a colossal spider with eight legs. He was Crawler, the master of Spuder, known for his biggest network of web. He was black in colour with long hair all over his body. His big red eyes and saliva from his mouth was sufficient to keep intruders away from Mount Spuder. He walked slowly as he took each step and looked with his big white, round eyes. The small spiders all over rushed to safety as they did not wish to get crushed under his legs. He walked shakily as he had not walked for a very long time. It was sixty years ago when he stood on his legs and walked out of his cave.

"I can smell royal blood and hear the sound of fresh

meat," Crawler said in a heavy voice as he stepped out from his cave, and then continued, "am I invited for a feast today?"

He crawled on his eight legs, letting small spiders fall from his body who were crawling all over him, and then looked at Anagol. He turned his face and then brought his face closer to her to ensure if it was really her. On hearing the wails, he shifted and looked and realized that the sound was coming from a baby wrapped in Vanadium.

"Oh! My pleasure to have the Queen of Electon," he said and took a step back, turned, and continued softly. "I knew this day would come." He paused and then asked his spiders, "Bring both of them inside my house and ensure no one must bite them." He crawled back inside his cave followed by spiders who carried Anagol and her baby, holding onto each possible space on her body.

The baby wrapped in Vanadium stopped crying as hundreds of spiders took him on their back and crawled slowly to take him inside the cave, not letting him get hurt. His one hand was out of the wrapping and looked cute as it touched the back of a spider.

First Call

1st July 1991

"Rhythm, stop. You are running very fast, wait for me." Milla was shouting running behind Rhythm as he ran fast with a black handbag in one hand and his grey overcoat in the other, struggling with all the things that he was carrying.

It was a sunny day of summer in Finland and Rhythm was already late for the event organized by his company, Telenokia and Siemens. He was a network design engineer with the company and had worked day and night for this day. Milla, his girlfriend, knew how important this day was for him. She was a network solution engineer who was working with him and understood how much effort he had incorporated on this historic project.

Finland's Prime Minister Harri Holkeri and the vice-mayor of the Finnish city of Tampere, Kaarina Suonio, were all set to create history by making the first GSM mobile call. Rhythm had been awake the whole night testing and ensuring that the first call may get through without any glitches. He went to freshen up early morning and got late.

To witness the historic moment, a whole lot of crowd

gathered at the central part of Finland. Loudspeakers were installed so that everyone could hear the first mobile call. Press reporters gathered at the designated space and public was allowed only until a particular spot.

Rhythm and Milla reached the entry gate and presented their identification cards to the security in charge. The big fat in charge looked at them and tried to match their faces while Rhythm looked at him in agitation as he was getting late.

"You may enter," the guard said, and as the gate was opened, Rhythm rushed in, holding Milla's hand. The top officials of Telenokia and Siemens knew this would have not been possible without the specialized brain of Rhythm. He was not only the concept builder but knew the technical specifications by heart. His boss often said, "It looks like you are the son of Thomas Edison–the man who invented Analog Signals–because of which we are entering into a new era of the mobile world."

He strode and reached the place where his other teammates were waiting. They both took a seat at the corner from where they could clearly see Harri Holkeri. Live commentary was going on on the loudspeaker and the crowd was cheering and applauding loudly. Harri Holkeri then stepped inside the car parked at the centre so that everyone could witness the moment. Rhythm then said to Milla, "My heart is beating fast. Can you hold my hand?" She smiled and held his hand. Harri Holkeri then dialled a number on the mobile to speak to Kaarina Suonio. As she picked up the call, the audience applauded, and a smile of appreciation and relaxation was visible on the face of Rhythm and Milla. Their hard work had been paid. They turned towards each other but that excitement was incomplete without the kiss of love. They all then stood up from their seats as Harri

Holkeri stepped out from his car holding a handset and then they continued to applaud. It was a big day for all of them and Finland.

Among the crowd, there was someone only interested in Rhythm and his eyes were only on him. Later, they had an office party to celebrate the success of their new invention and by late-night, Rhythm reached the lane of his house after dropping Milla.

Rhythm was a young boy, twenty-five-year-old, and parties always attracted him. He was known for his party fun and to be the one who forever stepped out last from a party. That night he had three glasses of beer and was happy as he stepped out from the taxi and started walking on the lonely lane to his home. He was carrying his bag in his left hand and his overcoat on his shoulder, humming a song, when he heard a sound from behind him. He could hear the sound of someone's footsteps on that lonely lane when he walked which got silent when he stopped. He turned back to check if someone was following him.

"Hello, anyone out there?" he shouted, but he could only hear his voice and the sound of bugs, which were all over the lamp post on the way. He waited for a reply and then again started walking. As he took a few more steps, he again heard the sound of footsteps, and this time he immediately turned to check but to his surprise, there was no one. He waited for a few seconds looking around and was shocked as he turned back and found his uncle, Goard. "You shocked me, uncle!" Rhythm said, bug-eyed, and walked by his side.

"Really? I am in shock since you came into my life," uncle Goard replied, with no expressions on his face. Uncle Goard was in his sixties and so fair that in winters, his cheeks went pink. He had a brown moustache and was so fat that Rhythm had rarely seen someone fatter than him. His hairstyle had always been the same since birth with his hair covering his ears. He worked as security in charge and so he got the name 'Goard'. He then began to only live for Rhythm and his beers, which he drank the whole day. Once Rhythm questioned him, "Why do you drink so much?" and he simply replied, "Beer is my fuel to be with you to guard you."

Rhythm took the stairs to his room, which was on the first floor. Uncle Goard occupied the lower level as he could not climb stairs. He yelled from below, "If you are coming back from a party, just grab a pizza for me." Rhythm heard, banged the door, and said, "Whatever."

"Never bang a door on me. I'll come up and bang you else," he again yelled, to which Rhythm did not bother to reply. This was a daily routine for him. Twenty-five years ago, uncle Goard found Rhythm at his doorstep one morning when he was about to leave for work. He was about to hand him over to the local police but stopped seeing a letter placed in the wrapped cloth. The letter said: Time will come when destiny will crawl to him, be with him for that future.

He then looked all around and safely closed the door. Uncle Goard then left his job and spent the rest of his life to be with Rhythm. For five long years, Rhythm was not allowed to leave home and was in the safe custody of his uncle; this was the main reason Rhythm hated him but uncle Goard loved him a lot.

Rhythm threw his bag in his room, removed his shirt, and jumped into his bed. He immediately slept as he was tired. His room was small – it had a computer placed to the side, a basketball set at the corner, and his clothes all over. His bed had several floppies lying all over, and he slept over them, not feeling the pinch of plastic. A full moon was playing hide and seek between the clouds, which could be seen through the open window of his room in that dark night.

By two in the morning, when the night was dark and the dogs were barking, a shadow could be seen travelling towards their house. As it passed the lamp posts heading towards the house, the light turned off on its own. It feared to find a shadow that was blue in colour. Rhythm was lost in his dream when a blue light appeared at his window, turning all the walls of his room blue. That blue shadow then travelled through his window and a white man with an outline of glowing blue light appeared, standing before him. He smiled on finding Rhythm. He then turned and pulled a chair which was placed at the corner and took a seat, folding his right leg on top of his left. As he positioned himself and looked at the walls of the room, the walls started glowing like a movie screen as childhood pictures of Rhythm began to flash on the wall. Images and videos which had never been clicked.

Rhythm looked disturbed by the intense light in his room. The man with the blue shadow remained seated peacefully, waiting for Rhythm to wake up, and then Rhythm opened his eyes and pulled himself back on the bed in astonishment. He yelled, "What the hell is this? Am I dreaming?" He then turned to look at the man with the blue shadow who spoke: "No, you are not."

Bug-eyed Rhythm pulled himself back, leaning on the headrest of the bed in fear. "Yo! Yo! Who the hell are you and what are you doing in my room?" Rhythm yelled in fear and tried to run outside, opening the door. But it was a simple task for the blue shadow man to jam the door and pull Rhythm back to his bed using his electromagnetic force. Uncle Goard looked disturbed by the sound coming from upstairs, but he preferred sleeping and ignored the noise.

Rhythm was pulled back to the bed's headrest with his hands glued to the sides. Chagrined, Rhythm looked all over his wall and looked at all his childhood memories running in front of him without blinking.

"What is happening? God, I am sure I am in a bad dream," he again yelled. Hearing him this time, the man gave a radiant look and replied, "I am Markboo."

"Who the hell, Markboo? You look like a ghost."

"Do I?" He gave a roguish look and then continued with a smile, "I am most loved in the future. People are crazy for me, especially girls."

Rhythm gave a quizzical look, "Are you some alien from another planet?"

"Not exactly. But yes, from another world which is the mirror of this world and the future of this world." Markboo gave a weird reply because of which Rhythm looked totally confused.

Markboo then stood up from his place and walked towards Rhythm and looked in his eyes. "Stay away from me, you look bloodthirsty," Rhythm shouted.

With a roguish smile on his face, Markboo reached next to him, and then looked at the chair which moved on its own to him. He retook his seat and said, "I am Markboo from Electon."

"Now what the hell is Electon? Is it in Europe or the US?"

Markboo then laughed out loud and continued after a pause, "You are an engineer or precisely, a telecom engineer. Let me explain to you in a better way."

Markboo then stood up from his seat and faced the front wall. He moved his hand in front of him and all the pictures which had been appearing previously vanished and a mobile tower appeared; the same mobile tower which Rhythm installed for testing the first mobile call.

"Hope you remember this?"

"It's the first base station tower which my team installed."

Markboo then turned to him and further questioned, "So how do mobile signals travel to mobile?"

Rhythm looked puzzled and felt as if he was getting interviewed. "Through electromagnetic radiations."

"You are intelligent." Markboo appreciated him and retook his seat. "Can you see electromagnetic radiations?"

"Not at all," Rhythm replied confidently.

Markboo now gave him a fixed look and said, "Common man cannot." He took a pause and then continued, "Electon is the world of electromagnetic radiations. It's another world which cannot be seen by a common human being," he paused, "but it exists."

"Are you from a team of Spielberg?" Rhythm questioned.

"Who is Spielberg? Anne Spielberg? Arnold Spielberg? Larisa Spielberg?" Markboo started taking names of different people with the Spielberg surname and as he called out names, their pictures began appearing on the wall. Rhythm got confused and then stopped him as he shouted, "Steven Spielberg." Rhythm then gave a chagrined look and said, "Who the hell are they?"

"You want me to share their details? I can."

"No. No, it's perfectly fine." Rhythm stopped and then said, "You continue."

"Continue about Spielberg?"

Markboo gave a coy look. "Your Electon story."

Markboo then paused, tried to recall his words, and

continued, "Heinrich Rudolf Hertz created Electon in the eighteenth century."

Rhythm now laughed and said, "What a story you are narrating? He was a great physicist who discovered electromagnetic waves and the unit of frequency 'Hertz'."

"Exactly! But in your world." Markboo came closer to Rhythm, made eye contact, and then continued, "In the human world, he created a unit of frequency and discovered electromagnetic waves, but virtually, he created a world of electromagnetic waves. Electromagnetic waves existed before too, but Thomas Alva Edison combined these two worlds when he developed analog signals and lit the first bulb. Due to his invention, electromagnetic waves started travelling to the human world, and we got a way out from the virtual world we were living in."

Rhythm gave an inscrutable look, and then he laughed out loud. He said, "You are a funny dude." Markboo gave a pained look hearing him laugh and was waiting for him to stop, but Rhythm was not able to control his laughter, and then uncle Gourd yelled from downstairs.

"Rhythm, what the hell are these sounds you are making in the middle of the night? Are you over drunk?"

Rhythm turned his face towards the door and shouted, "Nothing uncle, you go and sleep."

But as Rhythm turned back, the room was again dark. Markboo was not in his place, with no blue lights and no pictures on the wall. Peering, Rhythm pulled himself out of his bed and rushed to the window and looked everywhere for the mysterious man.

"Hello, Mr. Markboo? Where are you?" He waited for a reply and then turned back to his room, and then again, after a pause, he checked: "Mr. Storyteller? You are afraid of uncle Gourd?"

Rhythm was confused as to where had Markboo vanished. He got into his bed and within no time, slept again. He was confused if he had seen a dream or was it real.

A Damaged Mobile

Rhythm opened his eyes on hearing the birds chirp at his window in the morning. Uncle Gourd was playing the song 'sailing' by Christoper Cross on his tape recorder, and on hearing it, Rhythm knew that uncle Gaourd was making breakfast as it had been his daily routine for the past twenty-five years. Rhythm was not blinking while looking at the ceiling of his room, trying to recollect if he dreamt it all or did he really meet an alien named Markboo.

In the morning laziness, he got up and moved to the window of his room and looked around. He could still hear the same song being played again and again and the sound of the toaster and kettle. He started humming along as he knew this song by heart having been hearing it since his childhood. Nothing had changed in his house or with uncle Gourd in all these years.

He then walked inside his washroom to get ready for his office. Uncle Gourd was busy making toasts and spreading butter, cheese, and jam over them. Uncle Gourd was a big, beefy man with hardly any neck and a large grey moustache. He tried to move his legs slowly to the song, letting his big loose belly to shake. Almost daily, few loaves of bread got wasted because he dropped them and could not pick them due to his extra-large stomach, and this was a treat for the cat, Concha, which sat at his window every morning.

"It's another one for you, Concha. Take it away," uncle Gourd said in agony as one more bread dropped and Concha jumped to grab it. He then walked to the dining table and yelled to call Rhythm, who was having his shower.

Rhythm was standing under the shower, lost in the incident that happened last night. He almost believed that it was a dream until he saw a blue mark on his chest. Pallid, he looked at it in astonishment and then took some more soap to rub it off. He looked peeved because the more he rubbed, the brighter it got. He applied some more soap but with no luck to remove it. That stain started bothering him and left a substantial impact on his beliefs. He turned off the shower, dried himself as fast he could, and rushed outside to put his clothes on. He picked up his bag and rushed out, opening the door. Uncle Gourd looked up as Rhythm ran down the stairs. He shouted, "Crazy boy, you will bury me under this roof only one day."

"Good morning, uncle Gourd," Rhythm replied, opening the main door in a hurry. Uncle Gourd tried to pull himself out of the chair in which he was seated and then shouted to let his voice reach him. "Am I a fool making these toasts here?"

"Love you, uncle," Rhythm shouted as he ran towards the bus stop to catch the public transport. As he left, uncle Gourd peered and looked in suspicion at the first floor. He then decided to take the unconventional path, which he had not sought for the last thirty years. Although the space on the stairs was not sufficient to carry him, he tried taking small steps, turning right and left to fit his massive body and dragged himself to the top. He got exhausted as he reached the top and took a deep breath, collecting as much energy as he could and then opened the door.

Everything looked perfect as he tried to glance at each corner with his suspicious eyes until he closed them, spreading his hands to the side and took another deep breath to inhale. He waited for a minute as if trying to smell the intruder in his house, and then his eyes opened wide in shock.

Rhythm reached his office and was surprised finding a small cake party to celebrate the success of the first mobile call. Everyone had gathered around a table which had a cake placed at its centre. Everyone had a smile on their face and were proud of what they had achieved. Rhythm's boss was at the centre and had a big smile on his face, narrating the achievement and praise they had received worldwide. Rhythm slowly tried to peek into the crowd looking for Milla, who was busy clapping, standing in the front row. He tried moving amidst the people gathered, excusing them, and tapped Milla as he reached her.

"Hey! Rhythm, I was waiting for you to join," Milla replied in pleasure, looking at him.

Inscrutable, Rhythm pulled her by her arm and said, "Leave all this, I have something to show you."

"What? I need to have this yummy cake," she said but was dragged by Rhythm as he turned and pulled her along with him away from the crowd. He continued walking fast, holding her, while she kept on suggesting that they join the party and talk later. But Rhythm looked adamant about having a word with her. He kept holding her while looking for an empty meeting room and then pulled her inside.

"I need to tell you something very urgently," Rhythm

said, closing the door.

"Okay! Okay! Calm down," Milla said and pulled a chair.

"Tell me what happened?"

He gave her a look and then started speaking thoughtfully, "Look, you may find it weird but it really happened. Last night when I was sleeping..." Rhythm stopped, looked tensed as he was worried if he would seem to be a fool in front of her, but then continued, "my eyes opened due to a sudden light in my room, and I saw my childhood pictures floating all over the walls of my room and a man standing near me."

"I missed my cake because of your dream?" Milla said, interrupting.

"No. No, I wasn't dreaming." Rhythm took a seat next to her and brought his face closer to her to make her believe him. He then paused, looked into her eyes, and continued, "His name was Markboo; he was blue in colour and he explained to me that he came from another world named Electon."

He knew she did not believe him, but he preferred telling her anyway. "It's a world where technical things which we study are real and they look like humans but have powers."

Milla kept looking at him quizzically.

"He said that Heinrich Rudolf Hertz created Electon, which is a world of electromagnetic waves, and Thomas Alva Edison gave an entry path to these characters to the real human world by creating a bulb."

He paused, continued looking at Milla who was smiling while trying to hide her face, and then pretended to be serious and replied, "Rhythm, you need a break. You have been working day and night for this first call and have not slept for days."

"No, that's not the case. It was real."

Milla now placed her hands on his shoulders to calm him down, and then said, "It was just a dream, Rhythm. Sometimes when we are very tired, dreams may look very real. It's just the same and nothing else."

Rhythm knew she would not understand; no one would believe him. He remained seated and placed his hand on his forehead, giving a sour look, while Milla stood up, saying that she did not want to miss the party. As she turned and opened the gate, Rhythm called her again from behind. As Milla turned, she saw Rhythm standing without his T-shirt, and she got shocked, seeing a blue colour rectangle on his chest.

"So you wanna say that some alien is behind you?" Milla asked, sitting in a cab, as they decided to see a doctor.

"I do not know. I am clueless."

They soon reached a nearby clinic where the doctor asked Rhythm to lie down and started looking at the mark on his chest. The doctor looked at it carefully, avoided touching it and then started writing a prescription after taking his seat.

"So, what is it, doctor?" Milla questioned.

He thought and then replied, "It seems to be some sort of skin infection. I have given medicines which may help."

Although Milla looked convinced, Rhythm knew it was not a skin infection. He now wanted to know more about Markboo and Electon and was waiting eagerly for nighttime to arrive. He was sure that he would re-encounter Markboo.

Milla suggested Rhythm to go home early and take rest because he looked tired. He immediately agreed as he wanted to search his room to find some clue about last night which could prove him right.

As he knocked at the door, Uncle Gourd opened it immediately and pulled him inside in a rush. "Hey Uncle, what happened? Why are you pulling me in so hard?"

Uncle Gourd looked worried as he closed the door immediately and gave a wary look. Rhythm was shocked looking at the house, which had been sealed with iron bars and metal plates by his uncle. "What is happening, Uncle? Why have you sealed all the windows and doors?"

Uncle Gourd gave him a tensed look, and then Rhythm looked at him from top to bottom to ask, "Have you lost a few pounds, Uncle?"

Rhythm looked at him from top to bottom, as he could see his Uncle be more attentive and fit. Even his clothes looked loose.

"You hardly look at me. I am the same," he replied.

"But you have not answered me, what is happening?"

Uncle now turned towards him and took hold of his shoulders with both his hands and asked, "Tell me what happened last night? Who came to meet you?"

Rhythm looked puzzled as he had not conveyed about the blue man to uncle.

"How do you know about it?" he questioned, throwing his bag aside.

"It hardly matters. Tell me what happened last night." Uncle Gourd glowered this time and his voice was loud. Rhythm understood something was bothering him and he felt it better to tell him everything. He requested his uncle to take a seat and gave him a glass of water and then explained to him everything that happened last night.

Uncle had his eyes wide open while hearing the

entire incident and then he said, "For the next few days, you will not be going out of this house. No more opening of the door or removing metal plates from windows. You will remain inside the house till I find a solution."

"That's impossible, Uncle. I need to go to work and meet my friends," Rhythm said in a loud voice and then continued, "and who is this Markboo? What does he want from me?"

Uncle looked in his eyes and replied, "A time will come when warriors from the past will come to answer you and will help you fight against the dark world of the future."

Rhythm smiled, gave a quizzical look, and then after waiting for a moment, replied, "Till then, I am not ready to surrender my life and freedom. I am going to a party." He stood up from his place and moved to open the door. But before he could touch the latch, his uncle pulled him rashly and threw him on the sofa placed in a corner. Rhythm flew in the air and landed safely, in shock.

"I am Gourd and a guard who will not let you move out of this place. Better listen to me because I am your uncle, who lives to guard you against the dark world of the future," he said, coming closer to his face in anger.

Rhythm was confused as he had never seen his uncle in such an angry state. He always believed him to be the laziest person on this planet but the way he pulled him proved his belief wrong. He decided it to be better to run away when he would be sleeping than have a conflict with him now.

"May I go to my room or do I need permission from you even for that?" Rhythm questioned, showing his agitation. Uncle moved a step back to give him space.

As he climbed the stairs, Uncle said, "Remember son, I am not your enemy, but your friend for life." Rhythm ignored him and entered his room.

It was dark in his room as the window had been sealed. He tried to switch on the light, but to his surprise, it was not working. He looked up to check the bulb but was astonished to find that the bulb had been removed from the lamp. He looked around and then opened the door again to call Uncle.

"Uncle, who removed the lights from my room?" He was confused as he knew that his uncle would never climb to the first floor, but he was shocked to hear him say, "It was removed by me. Candles are placed in the drawer, light them up."

Rhythm was angry as he was not able to understand anything. He banged the door, picked up the receiver of the phone and looked frustrated on finding the landline dead too. He threw the receiver in anger and then jumped to his bed. He kept thinking about the incident and tried to link everything, but in vain. After a few minutes, he stood, lit a candle, and tried searching his room to find something about Markboo. After spending hours searching for a clue, he got tired. He sat back on his bed and felt isolated. But then he remembered that he has been carrying a damaged test mobile phone in his bag. Before testing for the first call, his team had assembled a few test handsets and one was in his bag, which he had been trying to repair last day. He immediately grabbed his bag, which was lying near his bed, and got the mobile. He stood up and moved to the study table and placed his phone under the light of the candle. He then started repairing it using the tool kit he had spread on his desk.

The room got darker as the sun went down and the light from the candle was sufficient only to light the area of his desk where he was working. He frequently kept changing the candles as they melted, but stayed focused on repairing the mobile as that was his only hope to contact Milla.

"Come down for dinner. I have cooked roasted reindeer meat with red wine," Uncle Gourd shouted from the ground floor. Uncle was all set to spend days locked in that house and so had brought the meat of reindeer, duck, chicken, all stored.

When uncle didn't receive any response from Rhythm, he looked up at his door and threw a spoon to knock at his door. That sound was good enough to distract Rhythm from his work.

"Coming," he yelled. Rhythm looked glazed as he placed the tool back, and after thinking for a second, he tried to switch on the mobile. But before the mobile could be booted, he heard the sound of another spoon on his door. With a frustrated face, he left the work he was doing and opened the door. He picked up the spoon and said, "Can't you wait, Uncle?"

Uncle Gourd didn't bother to reply while taking a bite of the meat. Rhythm reached the dining table and pulled his chair. "It's so pleasant to have a candlelight dinner with you, Uncle," Rhythm said sarcastically.

"My pleasure. We will have it daily," his uncle replied, taking a big bite from the meat. Despondent, Rhythm served food on his plate and was about to take a bite when they heard a sound from Rhythm's room. It seemed like something fell from his desk. "Might be the screwdriver I was working with."

But before they could conclude, another sound from the room had their attention, and a white and blue light started flashing from all corners of the closed door. The view was bright enough to illuminate the whole house. Chagrined, his uncle dropped the leg piece he was holding in shock while Rhythm rushed towards the stairs, shouting, "Markboo is back with my answers."

"Stop Rhythm," his uncle shouted and pushed his chair. He tried to grab Rhythm, but he was out of his reach and was already up half the stairs. Rhythm wanted to meet Markboo and get the answers to all the questions that had been floating in his mind. Uncle Gourd also rushed behind him, shouting, "He is dangerous, come back."

But Rhythm was not ready to stop and opened the door. He turned his face and covered it with his left hand because the light in his room was extremely bright. Uncle tried to reach him but got stuck on the stairs. He continued shouting to stop Rhythm but it was all in vain. Rhythm entered the room and got lost in the blue light.

Rhythm tried to look through the light but the light was so bright that it seemed like he was submerged in blue milk. And then Markboo appeared in front of him, wearing a black suit, glowing with an outline of blue light. He was smiling.

Rhythm looked at him with unblinking eyes and said, "You are real."

"No, I am an illusion of the human world but the past of Electon. Time to travel," Markboo said. "But I have a lot of questions for you," said Rhythm. Markboo smiled in his typical style and then turned towards the desk and picked up the mobile phone. He smiled and said, "Connecting worlds."

He then turned back to Rhythm and said, "Boo." Before Rhythm understood anything, his body started evaporating into minute pixels and began to enter inside the transmitter of the handset. "What the hell is happening?" Rhythm shouted but hardly heard anything as he swiftly moved inside the tiny holes of the transmitter. Markboo smiled, looked towards the door, and then quickly followed Rhythm, turning the room dark again which his uncle saw as he reached the second floor.

Uncle Gourd looked devastated as he knew what had happened. He stepped inside, picked up the mobile handset and gave a bleak look. Then he stepped outside the room and stood in the balcony to pull out a piece of bread from his pocket. He waited for a few seconds and then threw it on the ground floor, and Concha immediately grabbed it in her mouth.

Uncle Gourd understood that the time had come much before than it had been expected, and now he had to take some important decisions for Rhythm. He knew what he had been hiding from him since years, but he never expected that it would be the enemy who would expose him to the hidden truth.

Understanding Electon

"Welcome to Electon," Markboo said excitedly as Rhythm bumped on the ground of the lawn in front of his house.

Rhythm had no words and was puzzled and confused about what had happened in the last few seconds. He was trying to understand things. He immediately stood up and touched his body and pinched himself to feel that all that that was happening was real. He ignored Markboo and looked around. That place was new to him. It looked like a residential colony that had huge trees planted on the sides of the road and houses with a gable roof. Rhythm took a few steps and reached the street while Markboo remained aside, watching him. He knew it was something new for Rhythm. Rhythm looked to both sides of the road and then questioned, "What is this place? And why is it so silent?"

Markboo then walked confidently towards him, with hands in his pocket, and said, "This is Raritan Township, New Jersey, United States, Electon."

Rhythm looked confused, turned to him, and said, "Raritan Township? If I am correct, it was an old name of Edison township in New Jersey."

"You are correct, my boy," Markboo replied,

appreciating him. He placed his hands on his shoulder and within seconds, they vanished and reached inside the house which had been in front of them.

Rhythm looked confused and afraid of all that was happening. In a confused state of mind, he walked forward to take a seat on the sofa placed nearby. He placed his hands on his head in confusion. "I am bewildered and not able to understand what is happening with me?"

He paused and then shot an array of questions. "How did we reach New Jersey from Finland in seconds? How could I enter a mobile? Why is there no one in this township? What is this place? And why is it all dark here?"

For a normal boy who was living up to his dream of doing a good job and earn a handsome salary, this was all very confusing.

"It's natural and I was expecting all these questions from you," Markboo said and walked to take a seat on the sofa in his own sophisticated style of folding his legs one over the other. He continued looking at Rhythm, scratched his mild beard while Rhythm looked all around him to understand where he was.

"You are sitting on the same sofa on which once Thomas Alva Edison used to sit," Markboo said calmly.

"What?" Rhythm said in astonishment and stood up to look at the sofa and continued, "Thomas Alva Edison, the scientist who invented the bulb and many more patented things in the world of technology?"

"Yes, the same Wizard of Menlo Park; this was what he was known as," Markboo added, and then continued, "this is his house, where he established his laboratory for research in 1880, and after his name, this place was renamed from Raritan township to Edison township, which you humans call but we at Electon still call it Raritan."

Markboo then stood up from his place and walked to the window where a switched off bulb was hanging. He looked at it and said, "Rhythm, the time has come when you should know the truth about Electon because it's you who would lead Electon to its bright future and bring me and many others from the future to the present."

Rhythm stood up from his place and walked towards Markboo.

"What the hell? Someone else is also in this room," Rhythm shouted, as he saw a boy in the mirror. Markboo turned and observed calmly.

Rhythm moved in front of the mirror in which he saw a boy about ten years of age, wearing a blue jeans, white full sleeve T-shirt, with spiked-hair on the front and a spectacle with a black frame. Rhythm moved closer to have a look at this boy as it was dark, and the only light around was what Markboo was emitting from his body. As he moved closer, that boy also walked closer, and then Rhythm jumped back in fear as that boy was doing precisely what Rhythm was doing. Rhythm was observing his image in the mirror but as a child.

"Why am I not visible in the mirror?"

"You're visible, Roger," Markboo added patiently.

"I am Rhythm, not Roger," Rhythm corrected him. Markboo smiled and walked to him, saying, "Let me explain to you everything, Roger." Markboo then walked to the side of an open wall and started explaining to him with all the picture illustrations reflecting on the wall.

"It all started when Heinrich Rudolf Hertz invented electromagnetic waves in the human world. That day, a parallel universe called Electon that cannot be seen by humans got created. Anagol was marked as the Queen of Electon, whom you called analog signals in the human world."

He paused and looked at Rhythm and then continued, "Yes, the same analog signals in which current runs, but in this world, she is our queen, Anagol. Everyone was happy in her regime and there was always a bright sun in Electon. But then Thomas Alva Edison discovered bulb in the human world, which was a bridge between the human world and Electon. Everything was excellent and perfect until one-day, devil Noise travelled from the human world to Electon."

Rhythm immediately interrupted, "The same noise which is the technical term for the disturbance in mobile phones and handsets?"

"Yes, noise is an unwanted sound which is judged to be unpleasant, loud, or disruptive to hear. From a physics standpoint, noise is indistinguishable from sound, as both are vibrations through a medium such as air or water. The difference arises when the brain receives and perceives a sound, but in this world, noise is known as the unbearable Noise. Which is what he prefers to be called."

Markboo paused and flashed an image of Noise on the wall. He was tall, wore a white gown, and had long white hair with no eyes, nose, ears, or fingers.

"He is Noise. He cannot see or hear but can judge his enemy by his vibrations. He can make a sound so loud that it can kill all humans within seconds." Markboo paused and after looking at the picture for a while, continued, "As he entered Electon, he tried to be the Lord of the world. He wanted to be the king; he wanted disruption to be preferred and to rule Electon, he aimed to rule Anagol.

There was a massive war that happened when Noise

tried to capture the rule of Anagol, and he was on the verge of becoming the king when Crawler offered the peace treaty.

Crawler is the most intelligent among all of us and was always neutral for both parties. On the one hand, he agreed on Anagol to rule in the presence of Noise, on the other hand, he explained to Noise that the future is of Dslots and he can take them in his control from the start.

Somehow that war was frozen, but not the fight between Anagol and Noise. Anagol has been the softest queen, never tried to go against Crawler, but Noise was not the same. He always tried to harm Anagol and her people in some or the other way to extend his area.

And then, when Anagol had a successor, her baby, Noise decided to kidnap him as he knew he was the one who will be the entry gate to Dslots. Crawler tried to convince Noise and warned him that what he was doing was wrong and that he must stop, but Noise gained more power by that time and knew the intensions of Crawler. So he ignored him. This caused Crawler to take over Mount Spuder and he ordered all his followers that if Noise visits Mount Spuder, he must be killed forever."

"But who were Dslots?"

Markboo smiled and turned to him and said, "I am a Dslot." He took a seat and explained, "In the human world, you have seen voice calls or voice travelling through mobile phones or traditional phones using electromagnetic waves? They are all followers of Anagol who use sinusoidal waves to travel, but in the future, you will see pictures, messages, and videos travelling through mobiles. And that will happen by data slots." He paused and then continued, "In the world of Electon, this caste of people is known as Dslot."

Rhythm was listening to everything strangely, as he

had learned all these terms in his human world in books but never imagined them as people and that a world called Electon existed.

Markboo further explained, "Voice call always runs in a time slot, distributed in frequencies in the human world, whereas in the future of the human world, data will run over these time slots distributed in packages. Presently, in the human world, there's only voice call so there are Vslots in Electon. But in the future, data will get invented in the human world and we Dslots will come into existence in Electon."

"What happened to the baby of Anagol? Was he killed by Noise?"

Markboo continued looking at him, giving a blithe look and then said in a moment, "You are her baby, Roger."

Rhythm had his eyes wide open in surprise. "What? How can this be?"

"Anagol took you to the human world and requested Gourd to guard you and named you Rhythm in the human world, but for Electon, you are the future and successor of Queen Anagol, Roger."

Rhythm continued looking at him deadpan while he continued, "In the human world, you are twenty-five-years-old but you are ten-years-old in Electon."

Markboo now placed his hand on his shoulder and they moved to the terrace of the house, under the sky of twinkling stars. Markboo continued, "You are the future of Electon. You will bring a revolution. Time has come when Dslots be built for the future and it will only be possible with you. You are not alone in this fight, look around."

As Rhythm looked around, he saw a crowd of people dressed in black, with an outline of different coloured glowing light, walking towards the house of Edison. They were not in numbers to be counted. Where ever Rhythm's eyes travelled, it was people walking towards him. Green clouds above them were growing darker and denser, covering the twinkling stars, causing thunder and lightning to welcome Rhythm to Electon.

Rhythm turned to every corner to notice the gathering. He was staring wide in astonishment and fear, and then Markboo said in a loud voice to be heard by all, "We, the Dslots, welcome our king, Roger, to the world of Electon. Today we have gathered here from the future to greet him, but soon the time will come when we will be the reality. Say 'Like' in honour of King Roger." He then repeated again in a much louder voice to overcome the sound of thunder above, "Say 'Like' in honour of our King Roger."

And everyone raised their hands in respect. Leaning to say 'Like'. Seeing everyone at each and every corner leaning for his majesty, Rhythm walked to the edge of the terrace and climbed to have a look!

Everyone applauded in their own way by making a sound of Like, and then Markboo took a few steps towards Rhythm and said, "Welcome Roger, to your world!"

Although Rhythm appreciated the gesture and the respect that he was getting, he was worried thinking about Uncle Gourd. He was not sure if what was being said was real or just a story. But he remembered the words of his uncle who said someone will come from the past and will answer his questions about the dark world of the future. He was also thinking why his uncle kept it a secret from him and why he wanted to save him from Markboo. He was attentive as he knew it could be possible that what he had been shown was not the reality.

Being In Electon

"If Anagol is my mother, should we not go to meet her? She would help us?" Roger questioned.

Markboo gave a quizzical expression before answering him, and then he said, pained, "She is your mother, but the queen of Electon first." He took a pause and continued, "She knows that you are the power of Dslots and that your existence is dangerous for Vslots. She might not want to but she would be forced to kill you, to stop Noise from taking more power."

Roger was hurt on hearing this. He had a chance to meet his mother for the first time in his life.

"I don't believe it. A mother can't kill her son."

"If she can throw you to the human world, she can do anything," Markboo replied.

"But she did it for my safety?"

"She must have guarded you here, in Electon."

"But why then did she keep me alive? She must have killed me then?"

"She can't. She knew that it's because of your powers that Vslots were also getting energized. If she killed you, she would be left all alone." Markboo's justification looked like a perfect reply. When Roger was born, a new energy source called Frequency slot got developed in Electon. That energy source was in control of Anagol, which she used to enhance the powers of her fighter Vslots. That energy source was only because of Roger. It was said by learned people that if Roger dies, that energy source will dry out as it has been created because of the equilibrium of his enigma.

"So that's the reason Noise wants to kill me?"

"Now you have started to understand Electon's politics, my son," Markboo replied and then continued after a pause, "you need to be with me like a shadow, as every corner is menacing for you."

Roger thought for a while and then again questioned, "But if I am the energy source for the warriors of Vslots, she would not let me die. We should meet her."

"Hope this could be true, but I doubt it." Markboo looked in his eyes and explained further, "You were the energy source for Vslots about ten years back, but what is the status now, I am not sure. What if Vslots have found another energy source? Remember, the Electon world is not only on Earth, but it's also on many other galaxies and planets and they all are linked to each other. If in this duration they managed to find another energy source from some other planet, your existence is not important for her."

Roger listened carefully and remained silent as he was still trying to understand Electon.

Markboo took hold of his hand and said with a smile, "And remember, you are just a ten-year-old in Electon."

Roger nodded with his cuteness and asked, "So, what's next?"

"Hun! Next, we will travel to Seattle."

"And why Seattle?"

"Not only Seattle but Seattle in the future of Electon." And with a blink of his eye, they reached Seattle and stood in front of a lane which was densely crowded.

"This is the biggest shopping lane in Seattle called Detractor. Each day thousands of Dslots visit here to shop for their daily needs and many visit here for getting arms and ammunition." Markboo was explaining as he started walking down the lane holding his hand. The lane was narrow and had old shops from wall to wall. Rhythm looked at the paintings and the architecture sculpted on the walls. The pictures depicted Queen Anagol and there were massive sculptures telling the story of the history of Electon. Some shops had statues showing the Sun as a God fighting with soldiers, while some had beautiful sculptures of women. It looked as if that lane was the perfect reflection of Electon's past. As they walked, Roger noticed one common thing among all those shops–the candles. As it was always dark in Electon, each shop had candles as lights. The candles did not melt and their flame had different colours.

It was not just a single lane. There were lanes within pathways and each road was equally busy. As they walked, most of the people murmured looking at Roger; some even bowed to him.

"Why are they looking at me strangely?"

By then, they had reached the front of one of the shops. Markboo looked up at the story sculpted on its top. It was a lady holding a baby in her arms and black shadows trying to grab him.

"Because they know who you are and what's your purpose in Electon," Markboo said, explaining.

"Let's do some shopping," Markboo said and entered the shop. As they stepped inside, Roger questioned, "I have never heard about this place in the human world."

Markboo smiled and thought to explain to him, "You are in the future of Electon, and so you need to consider the future of the human world too." He paused and then continued, "In 1994 of the human world, a man named Jeff Bezos will form a digital shopping company called Amazon, in Seattle. That digital company will be the biggest shop on Earth in the future."

"So?" Roger questioned quizzically.

"Amazon is Detractor in Electon. You can shop anything you want from this lane," Markboo said, extending his explanation. "Each and every technical thing on Earth has its replica in the world of Electon, maybe in the form of a human or in any other form."

"Who are you in the human world?" Roger questioned, looking at him.

Markboo smiled and then replied, "In the future of Earth, in the year 2004, a young boy named Mark Zuckerberg will develop a social networking website called Facebook, which will be used to connect the world." He paused, smiled, and continued, "I am Facebook. With a name as a prefix of my lord, Mark Zuckerberg."

Roger thought for a second and then replied, raising his eyebrows, "But I do not have any money with me."

"You do not need money in Electon; you need encrypted codes."

Roger gave a vacant look. "You question a lot, Roger." Markboo gave a despondent look but then continued, "Everyone in Electon needs to keep themselves safe from the devil Noise, for which they need their soul to be encrypted. It's the same encryption as that which happens in the human world, where you encrypt a signal before transmitting so that the transmitted signal is protected."

Rhythm still looked confused.

"In Electon, depending on their status, people have encrypted codes available with them. You can say it is like a lifeline. If encrypted codes are finished, Noise will take over them and they will get lost in the space of Noise."

Markboo then raised his hand in the air and swept it gently, and as he opened his wrist, it had a bunch of numbers–zero and one's entangled to each other. He brought his hand near Roger and he looked at it ecstatically.

"These are encrypted codes. More of these we have, safer we are."

"But how to earn them?"

"It's simple but the toughest part. These codes are in the air of Electon; the wiser you are, easier it will be for you to grab them."

"Wiser means?"

"Everyone in Electon has their own importance, and depending on their position, they can grab these codes. Some people who are not so wise, do some business to get more codes to protect themselves and their families." Markboo explained and turned as he heard Mr. Dereck call them.

"Hello, Mark, pleasant to see you."

"Hey! Dereck. Long since we met." Markboo shook hands with him. Mr. Dereck was an old man. It was said that Mr. Dereck was two thousand years old. He was born in a year one thousand years before Christ in the human world. He welcomed Roger with his shaky hands and then greeted him by placing his hands on his head, saying, "Electon was waiting for you."

Dereck wore a long grey coloured cloth over his body, under which his wrinkled skin was playing hide and seek. His long white beard was a monument on its own, with hair spread all over his face as if it had not been made from years. He leaned a little, maybe because of his age, and then walked safely into his shop, which was all covered with dust.

"Sorry, Roger. This Solar dust is all over, and my old

body cannot clean it every day." Electon was in a cloud of dark cosmic dust from the extraterrestrial world that had entered Electon and the dust could be seen everywhere. "It's perfectly fine, sir."

"It's better to call me Dereck." He paused and then added, "Our future king."

Roger kept looking at him and then concluded, "I'll prefer to call you 'Sir'."

It was an honour for Dereck, and he smiled again and started walking further into his shop. His shop seemed to be an antique shop, with many unique things placed all over–some in shelves, some in bottles, some shining, and some dark.

"What is this?" Roger questioned, looking at red colour sand in a glass bottle. On hearing him, Mr. Dereck turned to check, "Oh! This is the sand from Mars. It contains oxidized iron dust, which has a property of resistance to corrosion."

Roger listened firmly and then questioned, "Where is it used?"

Mr. Dereck looked at Markboo, and they both laughed, saying, "Time will come, Roger, when you will need this." Mr. Dereck then started walking further, followed by Roger and Markboo.

Mr. Dereck then started searching among the hundreds of bottles placed on an old wooden shelf and then pulled out one bottle which looked as old as Mr. Dereck. It had white sand inside it. Mr. Dereck then walked back to the counter and poured some of that sand in a paper bundle and tightened it with buckles.

"This is for you, Roger."

Roger took that bundle in his hand, "Ouch! It's too cold."

"Yes! It's dust from Charon, a moon of Pluto. This

moon is the farthest in our solar system, and it keeps ejecting its cold dust to Pluto. Our Electon people, during the time of Maya Civilization in the human world, travelled to Pluto to collect the same. The new future will come when devil Noise would be taking over all of us. The dust of Pluto can keep his warriors away due to its resistance property."

Roger opened the bundle and took a little dust in his fingers, and felt the freezing sand.

"Pay the encrypted code, Roger," Markboo added. Roger looked at him blankly. Markboo then said, "Breath in through your mouth and exhale pressing your stomach, and then grab the exhaled air quickly."

Roger gave a peering look and did as explained by Markboo. The smile took over his face as he opened his wrist and found encrypted codes.

"Thanks a lot," Mr. Dereck said, as Roger handed him the codes and continued whispering in his ears, "warriors of devil Noise are all over. Keep this dust with you always."

As they left the shop, Mr. Dereck kept standing to look at him, and then he heard a sound in his shop from behind the shelf. He walked back and gazed. He moved slowly between the old wooden shelves, taking small steps, trying to figure out the reason for the sound. His eyes moved faster between the perfectly placed glass bottles. He then saw someone and was shocked to see a warrior of Noise standing behind the shelf. Mr. Dereck immediately took a few steps back, looking at the warrior who was wearing a black gown covering his head, with no facial organs. As that warrior took a step towards him, Mr. Dereck fell on his back in pain and fear. Black smoke was effusing from his body, as he said, "Noise will be angry, very angry with you, Dereck." Each step of his towards Dereck made Mr. Dereck slither.

A drop of sweat was evident on the forehead of Dereck as the warrior took slow steps towards him. With each passing second, Dereck's fingers were moving faster to unwrap the bundle of sand attached to his waist as he knew what he had to do to save himself.

"Time is coming when the force of slots will take your Lord to the dust," Mr. Dereck shouted and threw the dust of Pluto over him, making the warrior clamour which was enough to be heard by everyone in the lane. The dust particles pierced his body, turning him into a collection of the net. The black smoke could be seen coming out of numerous holes, and he vanished, blaring with smoke.

Roger, who also heard the loud sound, turned, but Markboo immediately grabbed his hand and vanished in an electromagnetic field.

They were again standing on the busy highway of Seattle. Cars, buses, and trucks were moving fastly. Roger was all confused while Markboo looked worried. He continued holding his hand, and then he said, "Do not leave my hand, whatever happens." Markboo looked up as purple clouds started taking over the sky.

"People in Electon drive cars?" Roger said, without knowing the danger which was approaching. Markboo looked glazed. He turned back to find black smoke balls shooting from the clouds and reaching towards Earth. The flying smoke balls were emitting fire due to friction in the electromagnetic field.

"Wow! Markboo, look, it's an amazing view," Roger shouted in excitement.

But soon, his excitement went away as those smoke balls converted into the warriors of Noise on reaching Earth. They were four of them, wearing a long black robe, covered from head to toe, and had no facial organs. They were wearing a knuckle punch on both hands. The knuckle punch was glowing purple, and Markboo knew the capability of that. Markboo moved a step and took Roger on his back, sliding him with his left hand. As he closed his eyes, his black attire started disappearing, and his body turned to a metallic sky blue colour, shining with white lines moving with a flare all over his metallic suit.

One after the other, those smoke balls hit the ground and warriors started walking towards them. Before Markboo understood their move, one of the warriors raised his wrist flashing his knuckle, and a flare of purple and yellow fireballs came towards them with the speed of light. Markboo took hold of Roger and twisted in the air jumping to the side and left a flare of blue light with his other hand towards the warriors. Another warrior pressed his right leg and took a leap in the air, jumping over Markboo, trying to burn him in his fire, but Markboo swiftly changed his position and threw a flare towards him, which took over that warrior, converting him into a net of smoke. That warrior then hit the ground, leaving dust and smoke. The three warriors were now glowering for revenge, became clangorous, and jumped in all directions to take control over Markboo. One of them yelled, "Give us Roger and you will be forgiven."

But Markboo was not in a mood to listen and threw Roger with his complete strength to a long distance. Roger got twisted, turned, and floated in the air before hitting the dusty ground. Markboo then looked at the warriors who encircled him, smiled, and said, "You are going to give another reason for girls to like me." He then took control of his body with his left hand and twisted himself in the air, floating his legs to hit the warriors. He then stood straight, ready for one on one combat. The warriors showed their grievance by making a wild cry and then started hitting Markboo from all sides using their hands and legs, but Markboo looked to be a perfect fighter. He was swift and was guarding himself against each of them, making strong moves. He moved his right leg back and with his right wrist, pushed one of the warriors, who got dragged to a distance over his feet. Roger looked at the combat from far and then ran to hide behind the pillar of the bridge. One of the warriors punched Markboo, resulting in Markboo to fly in the air and hit the windscreen of the car which was travelling at high speed. Consequently, many cars collided as they banged each other from behind, and then an explosion took place, causing a terrible fire and releasing smoke.

Markboo observed that one of the warriors was rushing towards Roger. So he took long steps and climbed over the cars, taking long jumps to reach before him. Other warriors followed him, jumping over cars and trucks. Markboo took a long hike to arrive in front of the warrior and said, "Aren't I better?" and gave a tight punch. As he turned, another warrior who was following him smashed his head with his left hand causing Markboo to fall on the ground. He got dragged and crashed on the sidewall causing it to break.

Markboo looked hurt this time as he pressed his stomach to sustain the pain. Roger peeped from behind the wall and looked haunted, as the warriors turned their faces towards him and started walking. Glazed, Markboo tried to stand back and when he decided to fire his flare, someone jumped from the bridge.

They were the forces of Anagol. Three perfectly figured ladies, dressed in red metallic suits tightened to their bodies, jumped with raised hands, folded right legs and straight left legs to land on the ground in front of the warriors. They looked stunning and had red eyeballs. All three of them took their position to fight. The confidence in their eyes was sufficient to scare the warriors. The warriors held their progress and said, "You are making a mistake, Vslots."

"And we love making mistakes," one of the red ladies said fearlessly. Hearing her, the warriors paused, turned to each other, and then flew back to the clouds as smoke balls. As per the agreement which took place many years ago between Noise and Anagol, they would not have a war again in Electon. That's the reason why the warriors of Noise left the battleground finding Vslots protecting Roger. They knew any action against the warriors of Vslots can only happen once Noise permits them.

Markboo was all set to fire, but she raised her left hand to freeze him, and said, "You know we love peace." She paused, while Markboo was struggling with pain, and then she continued, "You must return to the future."

She turned and started walking towards Roger when Markboo said from behind, "The future cannot be delayed by your actions, leave Roger." Hearing him, the red lady turned her face slightly, smiled, and didn't bother to reply. When she reached Roger, she went on her knees to bow and said, "Time to meet your mother."

Before Roger could have understood anything or called Markboo, he was taken away by those red ladies in a fire of red flames running in sinusoidal directions. Markboo kept standing, feeling lost.

Mother Anagol

The red ladies reached outside the palace of Anagol along with Roger. In the darkness of Electon, the castle of Anagol stood bright in purple colour on top of Mount Everest. The castle walls were the most powerful thing around them for miles, yet when Roger looked carefully, he noticed the stones. It was built of stones of varying sizes and shapes, each one unique. From a distance, it was a uniform purple, but when looked from up close, it was a mosaic of humble rocks. Nobody would have thought anything of them had they been left loose by the roadside. But together they were a castle, the crown of the landscape, and the protector of Vslots. It captured its own beauty as it stayed covered with snow all over.

"Where are we?" Roger questioned, stunned.

"Welcome to the castle of Queen Anagol. You are on top of Mount Everest," replied one of the red ladies walking inside.

"What? We are on top of Everest? No human has ever seen this?" Roger gave a quizzical look as he followed her.

"This castle is called Hertzonia and is a dream for Dslots and Noise," one of the red ladies explained.

The ladies walked forward, followed by Roger over the path covered with snow towards the massive door of Hertzonia. Roger had no words to say looking at the massive structure and was observing it with his eyes wide open. He was trying to understand each and every detail of Electon, which was a whole new world for him. One of the ladies then moved to the side wall where a bowl full of purple water was placed. She leaned to let her lips reach near that and then chanted, "Avalonia… a.a.a." She stepped back and observed the generated ripples in the bowl, and then a loud sound was heard as the door automatically started to open. That door was designed with multiple squares of various colours, and all squares began to shift their positions, making a loud noise. Those ladies looked at it calmly while Roger stood astonished as he looked at it bug-eyed.

"Each of these squares is a unique combination of frequency, multiplexed in such a way that if Avalonia is pronounced correctly by a Vslot, then the door opens," one of the ladies explained while walking inside.

"Is it only by Vslots?" Roger tried to know more.

"The sound of Vslots is inundated with time bands. A combination of time and frequency allows this gate to open," she further explained. Roger being highly technical by nature was more interested in it, and so he also added, "So if I am not wrong, as Noise does not have a time band in their voice, they can never get this door to open?"

She turned slightly while walking on the ramp of the arcade and said, "Perfectly said."

Roger looked highly influenced by the architecture of the castle as he looked around in surprise at the walls which were designed in extended rectangular frames, grey and purple in colour. Each frame was stuck back to back with small holes in them.

"Your castle designer must be highly equipped? What a design he has made."

The ladies looked at each other and then replied, "You may know the purpose of this design in the future."

They further walked to reach a sinusoidal path to the vast foyer. The foyer was expansive with four long pillars, each placed around the circle at the centre. The floor had sinusoidal lines starting from each of the pillars, juggled with each other, and ended at the thrones set between each space of the four pillars. The pillars had a complex design encrypted on them which resembled a deep-thinking circuit. Each line of the circuit had a glowing light in it making it look mesmerizing and interesting. As Roger closely looked, he noticed that the emission of light was because of the numerical digits flashing with a minute difference of time interval. It looked as if a maze of numerics appeared as per the logic registered behind it.

"Wait here, the Queen will be joining shortly," one of the red ladies suggested, and they stood surrounding Roger. Roger's eyes were still running all over as he was excited to find multiple things that he had never imagined. The red warriors stood with their hands straight, placed one over the other, waiting for Anagol to appear.

While he was busy in his own fantasy, those ladies suddenly bent down on their knees as they bowed with their head down and hands wrapped around the front knee cap. Roger looked at them stunned and was worried if he too had to do that, and then, from each corner of the foyer walked Anagol. Roger was surprised and turned in all directions to find four identical Anagols walking inside, saying the same sentences. It looked as if it was a mirror image of one. "You have grown up, my boy." Anagol looked at Roger wide-eyed and continued, "I left you with Gourd to save you from the evils of Electon." She paused, and with a blink, all four Anagols reached Roger, surrounding him from all sides and continued, "But these traitors cannot let you live calmly." Roger looked worried and brooded as the Anagol in the front cupped his face in her palm and kissed him on his forehead. Roger opened his closed eyes and saw that all the four Anagols had taken a seat at the four thrones placed at each corner. He turned to check them all. All four of them spoke at the same time and had corresponding content, and when she spoke, the sinusoidal lines started blinking from the thrones and hit the pillars to create an echo sound like one.

"So, you are going to kill me, Mom?" Roger said confidently, as he believed Markboo's words.

Hearing him, Anagol smiled and said, "And this must have been told to you by Markboo?" Roger gave a confident look to agree.

"This is what he wanted you to believe to benefit Dslots," Anagol replied with a sarcastic smile, and then continued after a pause, "can a mother kill her blood?"

"I know I am someone who can be a window to Dslots and you may not allow that."

With a gazing look, Anagol replied after a pause, "If Vslots need to be saved, any sacrifice is small."

Roger kept looking into her eyes and understood that Anagol was the Queen of Electon and not more than that for him. After a pause, he said, "Can you please send me back to the human world?"

Anagol stood up from her throne and walked towards him to say, "I hope I could. But you are not safe there as of now." She paused while Roger looked at her confused, and then she continued, "You need to learn to save yourself and fight against Noise because if you are killed, the existence of Electon would be over."

"What about Dslots? Am I safe from them?"

Anagol looked at him deeply to reply, "They are the future, not the present. And it's the responsibility of the present to create their future." Although it was not so clear to Roger, he was sturdy about his thoughts.

Anagol then turned and moved in front of her throne and continued, "You need to go along with your Uncle Gourd, and he will explain everything." Anagol had planned everything for Roger. She knew what was necessary for Electon and so, she called Gourd after Concha informed Anagol about the kidnapping of Roger. From the side of the first pillar walked a handsome, physically fit man. His body curves could be seen over the overcoat that he was wearing. Roger looked at him in astonishment, "Uncle Gourd, you look so fit."

Uncle Gourd smiled and hugged Roger as he rushed to hug him.

"I missed you, Roger," Gourd said. "I missed you too, Uncle."

Uncle Gourd bowed to Anagol and said, "It's my pleasure to serve you."

Anagol smiled with a confident blink and then replied to Gourd, "You have done a wonderful job Gourd, by protecting Roger for such a long time in the human world. Now it's time that Roger understands the life of Electon and be a part of us." She paused and then continued, "You know where you need to take Roger."

Gourd took hold of Roger to walk inside the castle. Roger smiled and confidently walked with him after saying goodbye to his mother. As they started walking, Roger smiled to ask his uncle, "You get beer in Electon?"

Gourd looked doleful and then replied, "That is

what I miss the most from the human world."

They both started laughing and started to chat while they entered the path of Electon.

Welcome To Hertzonia

Uncle Gourd took hold of Roger and walked to the backside of the foyer. They walked about fifty meters of the courtyard to reach in front of the enormous wall. That wall had a painting of Thomas Alva Edison. The painting dominated the walls, every colour was bold and painted with such precise lines that it almost looked like a mosaic. They were curved yet sharply defined; they seemed to be stable but could tumble at the same time. The scene painted was that of when Thomas Alva Edison invented the bulb; his face was at the top of the wall, almost touching the ceiling, and the bulb which he was holding with a wire was hanging at the bottom. The painting was done in bright oils, but somehow it was still dark. The painting looked like ash from some dirty fire had been mixed in. The paint itself looked like it was too thick on the application, giving the surface a rough look–the appearance of a stormy ocean. Every aspect of the painting conspired to bring your attention to the scientist who stood to hold his invention. Everything on that wall was painted, except the light of the bulb which looked real.

Uncle Gourd reached in front of the bulb and said, coming near to it, "Avalonia..a..a." As he finished whispering the word, ripples began in the massive wall. The wall which was made up of hard rock was shaking. Thomas Alva Edison, who looked to have been painted before, now looked more real. Roger took a step back, looking towards the top with his head gazing upwards. The bulb which was glowing until then switched off, and a passage got created within it. It was a small black hole of the size of the bulb. Nothing was visible on the other side except darkness. Uncle Gourd smiled looking at it and said, "Let's go inside, Roger."

Roger replied, glancing, "In this hole?" Inscrutably, he continued with a quizzical look, "It's too small for me to enter, I doubt even if my fingers can go inside?"

Uncle Gourd smiled looking at him and then said, "In the world of Electon, size is not salient. It's the power that needs to be judged." He paused and then continued, "Let me show you and then you follow."

Uncle Gourd was big in size, almost double of Roger in Electon. He turned towards the wall and first inserted his palm and then pushed his full hand; he then placed his head over the black hole and pushed inside. Now only his left hand and body below the neck could be seen to Roger. He smiled finding it funny, and then with a jerk, Uncle Gourd entirely vanished in the hole. It was now Roger's turn, and he looked tensed and excited to try that out. He wiped his hands and looked around to hide his nervousness. Roger took a step forward and placed his hand in the hole and then his head jerked to the other side. He fell on the other side over his head and then turned to slip over his back.

"You will learn too to cross this Alva hole," Uncle Gourd said, smiling, and gave his hand to Roger to stand.

That particular black hole was known as Alva hole in Electon. It separated the castle of Anagol with the other part. Most of the warriors were in the first part to protect Electon from intruders. Alva hole was a region of spacetime exhibiting gravitational acceleration which was so strong that it could compress anything of any size. The boundary of the Alva hole from which passing was possible was called the Alva horizon. Alva horizon was designed to detect and analyze the person entering the black hole.

The other side was discrete and inconceivable. Roger reached the vast green field between the enormous mountains. The thick forest lined up all around the green area. Roger could only say 'Wow' looking at the beauty. The peaks of the mountain could be seen reaching above the clouds and there were trees tall enough to make it look more mesmerizing. The long grass on the mountain was moving in the same direction as the wind.

"This place is known as the Arch of Electon," Uncle Gourd said.

"Let's go, we must reach on time," he said and continued to explain to Roger as he walked, holding Roger's hand.

"Arch is the area where all Vslots live, safely protected from Noise. We need to cross that forest and then we will reach Arch Rotunda."

"Is it some hotel?" Roger questioned.

Uncle Gourd thought for a while and then asked, "Tell me what is a time slot in the human world?"

Roger was well aware of that, and he immediately answered, "In mobile technology, there are multiframes which are 120 milliseconds long. Each multiframe has twenty-six frames which are 4.6 milliseconds long, and each frame is divided into eight-time slots, which are 576 microseconds."

"Exactly," Uncle Gourd said and continued to explain. "In Electon, female Vslots are the multiframe who have the strength of one hundred and twenty Avalonia, males have the strength of forty-six Avalonia, and kids have the power of five Avalonia."

Roger stopped and gazed at his uncle puzzled; this was good enough for Gourd to understood that he didn't understand anything.

"Okay, let me simply explain to you," Uncle Gourd

said and then continued. "Vslots and Dslots are actually time slots of our human world. We will not talk about Dslots as they might come in the future, but they do not exist now.

In Electon, these time slots are the same as the human world's; they have husbands, wives, and children. About five hundred million years ago, there was a tectonic plate that was an independent continent called Avalonia. It was the most active tectonic plate of Earth, and so the powers of Vslots are measured in the unit of Avalonia.

As female Vslots are stronger, they have more Avalonia than males, and kids have the lowest."

Roger tried to understand and then interrupted, "That means females have higher chances to win over Noise than the males do and so that's why it was the red ladies who were warriors of Queen Anagol?"

"You got it, Roger." Uncle Gourd continued, "Arch Rotunda is a place where all kids of the Volts live so that they can be guarded safely from the reach of Noise. The devil Noise knows that attacking adults with more Avalonia is sturdy, and kids with lower power are an easy target. Our Queen got this Arch Rotunda constructed for the safety of the kids."

"You too live in Arch Rotunda?" Roger questioned.

Uncle Gourd smiled and said, "I am not a time slot. I belong to a community that is supposed to guard Vslots. We are in many numbers, and each Vslot kid has one guard attached to them for their safety." He paused and then continued, "It is a long story, maybe some other day, but I was chosen for you. We all guards keep an eye on the Arch Rotunda from outside."

"When did you come back from the human world?"

"I got called," Uncle Gourd said desolated.

They soon crossed the green belt and reached the dense forest. Roger was wandering through the woods of his dreams. He listened to his feet tread, the twigs, and leaves which were cracking under his feet. A smell of timidness hovered in the air... no one had a clue of what lay ahead! Clutching Uncle Gourd's fist tightly, Roger kept moving forward.

"This forest has its own story," Uncle whispered while walking, "any member who gets punished by the members of Electon is brought to this forest to be beheaded. It has the dark sound of dead souls who try to speak to you as per the reason they had been punished." They walked fast. Roger started hearing whispers below his feet as if many people were trying to whisper in his ears. Roger tried to clean his ears and even turned back to see if someone was there, but Uncle Gourd asked him to ignore all the sounds and keep walking fast. He explained that these sounds have the power of illusion which could keep you stuck in the forest for life.

"Anagol would kill you."

"Go to Dslots. They need your help."

"Lord Noise is a wonderful character, go and meet him."

Many such whispers tried to stop Roger, but Gourd took hold of his hand to drag him to the base of the snow-covered mountain of Arch Rotunda.

"There it is–Arch Rotunda." Uncle Gourd showed Roger a massive structure on the top of the snow-covered mountain. It had many domes with walls made up of massive stones. Each stone was in a rectangle shape with various pillars at each corner of the structure.

"From here onwards, Ber will take you to the top."

"Ber?"

"They know precisely the error between the time and distance and how many bits needed to be travelled as per your weight to the top. Reaching Arch Rotunda is not for everyone. Ber are very aggressive and short-tempered creatures. If they are with you, your aim will always be precise without any error. Our warriors use them to calculate the error when arms are fired. Everyone respects them."

Roger looked worried as Gourd asked him to walk further to reach the Ber station. Roger first started taking slow steps and kept turning back to look at Gourd. His legs submerged in water up to his knees as he crossed the small river in between. He was surprised as his wet trousers dried on their own when he placed his foot back on the ground. That was the beauty of that small river. It created an illusion of water although it was the flow of cosmic waves that Electon received from the extra-terrestrial world. He looked up at Rotunda, which was playing hide and seek between the green clouds. He walked further and then turned again to look at Uncle Gourd. He was still standing at the distance and waved at him to continue. Roger walked and reached the wigwam at the base of the mountain. The wigwam was a small, dome-shaped hut made by fastening mats, skins, or bark over a framework of poles. Mostly, the wood used was dried and grey-black in colour. The door had a curtain that seemed to have been made up of a shiny element.

Roger slid the curtain to enter the wigwam but rushed outside in fear and fell on the ground.

"Can't you say may I come in please!" said one of the Bers as he walked outside on his two small legs. Ber are creatures who had tiny legs like those of a dog, thin waist like a snake, and a face that resembled that of an ant with big wide eyes and big ears like a monkey. His red moustache, which had precisely six hair, shook as he glared at Roger in anger. He wore a shirt with a black blazer on it, which hardly reached his hips. He wore a blue denim bottom until his knees.

Roger immediately stood up and touched his elbow which was slightly hurt due to the fall. He bowed in respect as he remembered what Uncle Gourd suggested about them. "I am extremely sorry, sir, and regret my mistake."

That Ber gazed at him and then said after a pause, "Roger, son of Queen Anagol." He turned and then continued, "Even the Queen needs to learn manners." He spoke and walked back inside.

Roger took slow steps, and this time, he asked for permission to enter. "Learning from mistakes is a good habit. Sign here." The Ber turned a book towards him.

The logbook was to enter the details of Vslots who were taken to Arch Rotunda. The book was old and heavy. Maybe it had been maintained since the beginning of Electon and had a living palm of someone attached to it. The fingers were long, with sharp dirty nails and bloodstains could still be seen near the line where that half hand was attached to the book. Roger looked tensed when the fingers of the palm started moving as he turned the pages of the book to write the entry.

"Do not worry about this hand. It's a hand of the first Sumerians, who lived around 4000 B.C., and who first discovered writing. In Electon, his hand still guards the logbook." The Ber then turned and shouted, "Number five hundred and sixty-six." On his call, another Ber came running.

"Who needs to be taken, my lord?" he questioned the Ber in-charge and then turned to look at Roger.

Roger immediately bowed to him and said, "My pleasure to drop you to Rotunda."

"Come with me," the Ber said and sauntered. Roger followed him confused. He removed his spectacles to clean it while he continued to follow him. The Ber soon reached the circular platform which was made of old grey metal with formulas encrypted on it. The old round metal plate was placed between the dark hard rocks, with a lot of leaves and grass around. Roger followed Ber, taking selectively safe steps. Something was engraved on that metal plate in a symbolic language that Roger did see but could not understand.

"You need to hold my waist tightly when we fly to the top. We will travel with the speed of light and may take a second to reach the top."

Roger looked at the thin waist and was worried if his waist could take his weight. The Ber stepped at the centre of the platform and looked at Roger with his big eyes and said, "Hold my waist tightly."

The Ber was too small and did not even reach until the waist of Roger. So Roger went on his knees petrified; with shaky hands, he tried to grab his waist. Roger was scared as the waist of Ber was so small that it could be clutched in the fist of his one hand.

"Hold it with both your hands," the Ber added. Hearing him, Roger nodded fearfully and placed his other hand on his waist. He felt as if he was holding a carrot in his fist. Roger then looked up and was further worried as he could not see the apex which was above the green clouds. He then closed his eyes as the Ber chanted, "Errorosia…" The metallic platform started to glow, emitting blue light and then, with a loud sound, the Ber flew upwards, releasing flames of fire from his feet. Roger shouted in fear and then opened his eyes to see that his feet were in the sky and that the platform was almost invisible. He kept looking up to ensure that his spectacles do not fall. Then, with a blink, the Ber landed on another platform at the top. Roger took a deep breath as he reached the top and adjusted his glasses.

"Your way is that way; I hope you enjoyed the travel?"

"Ya, thanks a lot, sir," Roger replied and then turned to look at the entry gate of Arch Rotunda. It was a wide gate with few stairs. The Arch had the perfect impression of Roman architecture. He moved towards the main entrance while Ber jumped back, making a funny sound: "Yahoo!"

Roger smiled at him and then walked towards the lady who was standing at the top of the stairs. She looked old, wore a long, deep purple woolen gown. She had long white hair. She looked strict as she stared at

Roger with her hands folded. Roger climbed the stairs and reached her. Before he could say anything, she said in a controlled voice, "I am the main station controller here and my name is Emma." She paused and looked straight in his eyes and then continued, "Arch Rotunda is what we call station." She took Roger inside the gate and covered him with a woolen sheet as it was cold due to the snowfall taking place outside. From the top of the cliff in that darkness, Uncle Gourd could still be seen at the same place looking above at Roger till the doors were closed again.

"You must be feeling cold, but not to worry. Change your clothes once you reach your room and sit around the fireplace," Emma continued to explain to Roger as she walked while holding him.

Roger's eyes were on the structure, which was magnificent and vast. With huge corridors, paintings, and Roman architecture, it was looking vibrant in the light of fire lamps placed at equal distance on the way. As they walked, the shadow of Roger and Emma could be seen on the front wall. It extended to the ceiling due to the reflection of light from the fire lamps. The corridors looked empty as if no one lived in that Arch Rotunda. While walking, Roger could only hear his footsteps and the sound of his and Emma's breath.

"May I interfere with the registration?" a croaky voice echoed from behind. Emma knew who it was, and she stooped to turn back. A middle-aged man with a thick moustache, long white hair which reached until his shoulders and grey eyes, stood with his hands in his pocket at the door of one of the rooms and looked at Roger in suspicion. He was wearing a black attire.

"Thought he could do his formalities in the morning, he is wet and needs warmth for now," Emma started walking towards that man and explained.

"Welcome, Mr. Roger. I am Greg, and in-charge of home location register maintenance for this Arch," Greg said, bringing his face closer to Roger.

Roger looked bewildered as everything was new and different for him. But he was readily accepting everything and following what was told to him, as he was just ten-years-old here and his thinking was as per his age.

"This Arch is our home and Mr. Greg is responsible for verifying and registering any new entry. He would also allocate a room to you," Emma explained.

"Thanks, Emma," Greg said in his croaky voice, and then continued without a smile on his face. It was noted in Arch that Greg last smiled when Thomas Alva Edison invented the bulb.

"You may be wet, Mr. Roger, and you are the son of the Queen, but Arch Rotunda has its own rules and I only have reverence for my duties," Greg exclaimed with a grave look and opened the long fat logbook which was placed on the table next to the fireplace.

Roger looked into his eyes and nodded. Greg then gave him a pen. Roger started filling the form for entry but then stopped at the entry which asked if he was a Vslot or a Dslot. Roger began to think about what he must enter in that field. Greg observed his face carefully and then said, "the son of the Queen of Vslots is confused?"

"Tick at the Vslots," Emma interrupted and softly guided Roger while Greg continued to look at Roger dubiously. As Roger finished the form, he started to get up from the chair but Greg stopped him and explained that after the form has been filled, the logbook will automatically assign a room to him based on the entry, his way of writing, his future, his present and his attitude towards Electon. Roger looked back in the logbook and then at the corner below the logbook, there was a block with black lines, in which a room number flashed on its own.

"Room number five hundred and seventy-six," Greg said.

"Thanks, Mr. Greg; I will show him his room," Emma said and took the permission from Greg to move, holding Roger, trying to cover him in the woolen cloth. Roger thanked Greg and walked along with Emma while Greg continued to stare at Roger from his room.

Emma took him to the lift area and pressed the up button. It was a lift completely made of glass which was not supported by any walls or strings. "*Which floor*?" an automatic voice in the lift questioned.

"Five hundredth floor," Emma said, in a loud and clear voice. The door closed, leaving Roger astonished.

"This building has five hundred floors?"

"No, your room is on the five hundredth floor. The total number of floors is twenty hundred," Emma replied soothingly.

"And how much time will it take us to reach there?" Roger questioned in anxiety.

"*You've reached your floor. Pleasant stay!*" the lift's automatic recorded voice said, and the door opened.

Emma looked at Roger, gratified. "The lift takes only 2.048 milliseconds to cross one floor." They started walking to the left of the lift area, and Emma was noticing the room numbers which were flashing on the walls digitally. Along with the room number, the picture of the room's owner was also fulgurated at the entrance. Roger was busy reading each name and glancing at the images when Emma stopped at one of the rooms.

"This one is your room," she said and knocked at

the door. Roger looked at the side of the door to check his roommate, and it flashed the name Cooper, with a picture of a young boy with his details. He was thirteen, American, and a Vslot.

"Hello, Emma, how may I help you," Cooper said, opening the door. He was a young boy, with medium-height, brown-haired, and he looked studious.

Emma placed her hand on Roger's shoulder and said, "Mr. Cooper, he is Roger and your roommate."

"Hey! Hello, nice to meet you," Cooper said, presenting his hands to greet and then continued, "please come in, brother."

"Mr. Cooper, being the elder one, it's your responsibility to take care of him and explain to him everything about Arch Rotunda. Be his buddy," Emma said.

"Definitely Emma," Cooper said and closed the door after thanking Emma as she walked back towards the lift.

Roger walked inside and glanced at his room. It was a small room with two beds at the centre and two study tables on the sides. It had a big window in the middle through which green clouds could be seen below.

"You may take the bed to the left." Roger nodded and looked at the books Cooper was reading.

"I am a humanoid," Cooper said, and Roger looked at him strangely.

"Humanoid means?"

Cooper took a seat on his bed and pulled a drawer to bring out sweets for Roger and said, "There are two types of Vslots. One who are pure Vslots and developed in Electon only. Others are humanoids who are born in the human world, and at the same time, their replica gets created in Electon as a Vslot."

Roger listened and then questioned, "So you exist in both worlds?"

"Yes."

"How lucky you are," Roger looked excited.

"No, it's not excitement. In the human world, my character does not know anything about Electon or me, but I know everything. Even the work that he is doing and what exactly he is up to."

"Isn't it good?" Roger replied.

"No, as Cooper in the human world is a mobile scientist, he keeps on inventing new pieces of stuff which are good sources of information for Electon, and I am used for that purpose. I am always at a high risk to be taken away by Noise."

"Hun, I can now understand but do not worry; I am here with you and will try my best to help you in all possible ways," Roger replied, smiling and continued, "by the way, who are you in the human world."

"I am Martin Cooper, an American Engineer. I am a pioneer in the wireless communications industry, especially in radio spectrum management, with eleven patents in the field. I invented the first handheld cellular mobile phone in 1973 and led the team that developed it and brought it to market in 1983."

"Oh my God, are you the same Martin Cooper who is 'the father of the cell phone'?" Roger asked, bug-eyed.

"Ya! The same, but it's all done by the Martin Cooper in the human world; in Electon, I am still just thirteen-years-old," Cooper said, making an annoyed face.

"Obviously, the development you are doing in the human world is what will be reflected in Electon. And tell me..." Roger had many more questions, but Cooper interrupted him, saying, "Roger, you must change now else you will get sick. And let's sleep. We will have a lot of time tomorrow."

Roger had many more questions, but he realized the time and went to sleep after changing.

It was difficult for Roger to sleep that night, being in a strange place that looked like a dream to him. He glanced at Cooper who was Martin Cooper in the human world and Roger's role model. While working in Finland for the first mobile call testing, Roger had read a lot about him and about his passion for mobile handsets.

Dslots Within

"Hey, where are we rushing this early?" Roger questioned, following Cooper, who was walking fast, wearing his formals with a tie, while Roger was in his formals but still adjusting his tie.

"Every morning, all Vslots of Rotunda need to gather at the common area on the ground floor. Administration of Arch Rotunda performs verifications and gives us the task for the day which will help us to stay safe from Noise and also help us to learn new ways to keep Electon safe."

"But that should be done by warriors and not the kids, right?" Roger further questioned, running behind Cooper.

"Who are warriors? We are warriors of our own. We need to be alert and alert Vslots if we find anything suspicious," Cooper explained and then reached the common area of Arch Rotunda.

The common area of Arch Rotunda was on the ground floor and was a big circle with a foyer on all of its sides and pillars at equal distance. The celling of the common area was covered with a screen on which various images and scenes were flashing. The screen was shiny like a mirror but was changing every few seconds.

Roger admired it for some time to understand the fourth-dimensional stories being flashed.

"The stories which are being shown above are some live highlights from the human world," Cooper said, bringing his face close to Rogger.

"Something like news channel?"

"You may say so but whatever is flashed is about us in the human world, in the form we existed in that world," Cooper confirmed.

Roger found it exciting and was also shocked to find thousands of kids lined up in front of the stage. Each kid was dressed similarly, wearing a white shirt and black trousers with a black tie and girls with a black dirndl. Cooper and Roger took the last position in the line.

"You are late, Cooper," the girl standing in front said, leaning slightly back to Cooper.

"Hope you mind your own business, Olivia," Cooper said, bringing his face near her ears. Olivia gave a bleak look and turned front.

Rogers's eyes were all over as he was trying to understand what was happening in there.

"Good morning, Vslots," the Head of Arch Rotunda, Noah said. Noah was appointed by Anagol to manage Arch Rotonda about fifteen years ago. He was a humanoid and born in the 19th century when James Clerk Maxwell was born in the human world. In the human world, James Clerk Maxwell was known for inventing the formula for the electromagnetic field which suggested that the electromagnetic fields can travel with almost the speed of light. He was twenty-five when he discovered about Saturn rings and concluded that those rings were made up of multiple particles which he called 'brick-bats'.

Only people of Electon know that behind the inventions of James, it was Noah who was his own replica from the electromagnetic world. As per the nature of the Electon world, after the death of James Maxwell in 1879, Noah must have died along. But he survived. Noah was only one humanoid in Electon who was still alive after the death of his human world replica, and it was a mystery for all.

Noah was always dressed in black attire with only a

white shirt inside and a black tie. He had cufflinks that resembled the alphabet 'E'. He had long white silky hair that reached his shoulders and a big white moustache. He wore big black spectacles, which went as a contrast with the colour of his hair.

He was not alone at the platform in front but was accompanied by other administrative bodies.

"We all Vslots know that future is coming to overtake our existence and that's the reason we are here at Rotunda, to ensure we save our future." He paused, looked at each one of them, and then continued, "It's sad that we are fighting with ourselves to save ourselves from the future which we do not expect, but we know we are dependent on the human world which is desperate to spoil its own destiny." Noah again paused and then continued in a soft voice, "You all need to be aware that you are not safe, not only by the future call but also by Noise who is trying it's best to reach Arch Rotunda."

Everyone in the crowd started murmuring. Noah paused and then said in a loud voice, "But you need not worry. Our guards are at work and they know how to keep you safe. Ensure that you do not leave Rotunda without administrative permission. For the special task, we will be defining the process and will ensure you all are safe."

He stared at all of them and then his eyes stopped at Roger, and then he concluded, "Before dismissing the assembly, I would like to ask Cooper, Olivia, Eva, and Roger to see me in my cabin soon after my statement." He paused, looked again at the astonished Roger and said, "Dismiss."

Thousands of children from ages five to seventeen dispersed. They started moving in groups, chatting, laughing, and discussing. It was a typical day for them, but many of them were keen to have a look at Roger as he was the son of the Queen. They had seen him in ancient stories and carvings in the hands of Anagol, but it was the first time he was between them as one of them.

Cooper started walking downcast, holding a book in his hand, thinking, which he always did. "Cooper, why does Noah want to meet us? Any idea?" Roger questioned, running behind Cooper who was walking quickly.

"I am not sure, come along. We will meet him," Cooper replied, still walking fast.

"We are supposed to meet him too, Cooper," Olivia interrupted him.

"It's unfortunate for me," Cooper replied to Olivia, giving her a bleak look and started walking.

"It's the same with me. My bad luck!" Olivia said and started walking fast, following him and then turned towards Roger, smiled and said, "Hello Roger, it is amazing to see you."

"Thanks and same here," Roger replied.

They reached the passage which moved to the cabin of Noah. Cooper was in the front, leading them, and the other two were taking quick steps to match his speed.

"Where is Eva? She should have joined us too," Olivia said, still walking.

"Sorry?" Roger said to Olivia.

"Eva? You do not know her? Do not tell me that," Olivia said, giving a peering look and continued, "she is the one about whom every boy of Arch knows, and you are asking about her. But I still feel I am more beautiful than she is."

Olivia was a Vslot whom Cooper hated as she spoke a lot. She could not keep her thoughts to herself and murmured them even when she slept. She was a beautiful girl with straight hair and a fair complexion. Cooper did a task with her in the future which failed, and he believed her responsible for the same.

They reached outside the cabin of Noah. His cabin was on the ground floor at the extreme corner of the Rotunda. His cabin was designed with big red bricks, which were said to have been collected from the rings of Saturn. A saying was engraved on the sidewall which said: "*Your future is what you do today, think and take action accordingly.*"

Cooper hit the brass gong placed at the entrance for permission. A resonating sound could be heard inside.

"You may come inside Cooper," Noah was heard saying from his cabin.

All three of them entered and saw Noah sitting on his chair on the opposite side of the desk. His desk was stupendous, with a model of Saturn placed at one corner and a hexahedron of shining silver colour on another. That hexahedron was changing its shape on its own. Behind Noah was a prodigious mirror that was crystal clear and the property of that mirror was that if any Vslot stands in front of it, his humanoid could be seen in the mirror if one had a replica in the human world.

From the position where Roger was standing, he could see Noah as James Maxwell and Cooper as Martin Cooper. He could not see himself as Rhythm as he was a pure Vslot and not a humanoid.

"Welcome Roger, to the Arch," Noah said in his croaky voice.

"Thanks, sir."

Noah was about to speak further when the gong resonated again. "Come inside, Eva." Noah could know who the person was without seeing who hit the gong because of the modulated frequency generated by the pressure on the gong. Each and every Vslot, when resonated with the gong, created a different ripple of sound frequency which Noah could decrypt in his mind.

Eva entered the room. She was a sweet, studious girl, with hair until her shoulders, blue eyes, and pink cheeks due to the cold outside.

"Sorry for reaching late, Noah," Eva said in her modulated voice.

Noah nodded and smiled. He took a few steps to reach the whiteboard, which was placed to his right, and then he murmured something looking at it. Soon a picture of a handsome boy appeared on the board. He was a tall, long-faced man who seemed to be an American.

"He is Mr. Bernhard Walke in Nysa, Poland. In the human world, he has done a lot of research work in mobile technology. As per our sources, he is now working along with his student, Peter Decker, on GPRS." He paused and looked at all of them.

"Sir, what is GPRS and how is it related to Electon?" Cooper questioned.

Noah moved back to his seat and then started explaining, "GPRS stands for General Packet Radio Service. Presently, the mobile system runs on analog signalling that is Vslots but he is trying to develop this GPRS so that data can be transmitted over electromagnetic waves. This technology would be the first step to bring Dslots into existence." He took a pause and explained further, "GPRS will be used in the human world to transmit information in the form of pictures and multimedia messages, which is Dslots." He again paused. "It will be an entry point of data slots in the human world and danger to the existence of Vslots."

"What's the problem if Dslots come alive?" Roger

interrupted with his question.

'Presently, humans use only voice calls in an electromagnetic field that is Vslots. As per Crawler, in the future, Dslots will take over the human world where they will be called GPRS, 3G, 4G, and so on. When Dslots come into their full existence, humans will become slaves to mobiles. They will keep these mobiles always with them; they will transfer images, videos, and many more things in seconds causing disruption and information bulging. They would also start using Dslots for voice calls, and soon, we Vslots will start dying from Electon as we would get erased from the human world, and finally, it would be only Dslots in the world. Slowly, they would take over humans and their brains and their coming generations, allowing the entire human race to end."

Roger looked at him with worried eyes. Noah then continued with a pause, "We need to stop humans from bringing Dslots now, else it will be too late." He looked at them with tensed eyes and continued, "In the universe, many planets from various other galaxies had faced this situation and we have seen planets dying after the extinction of humans. We do not want that to happen on Earth. Our job is to save this planet."

Roger nodded as Noah looked into his eyes.

"So, what is the task, Noah?" Eva questioned.

"You four need to travel to the human world to Poland and deflect Bernhard from his research. He must get so confused that he cannot invent GPRS," Noah added.

"Should we not kill him in one shot and finish the game?" Olivia said.

"You can't Olivia, as you are his humanoid," Noah said. Roger and others then looked in the mirror behind

Noah and saw Olivia as Bernhard behind the mirror.

"Holy shit!"

"If any of you killed him, Olivia would die too in Electon, and that we do not want under any circumstances. Olivia is the chosen one for this project as she has the benefit of reading his brain."

"But then how to stop him from his research?" Roger questioned.

"Divert him, create an obstruction or anything by which we can delay his research," Noah added.

"Can he see us?" Cooper questioned.

"He can see Roger as he is a true Vslot but not the other three of you. You can be seen by only Roger," Noah explained and then continued, "you may do your research before entering the human world for which you have three days. Your respective guards will accompany you, who will be in an invisible mode. Get ready and ensure that no one knows about this task except us five."

"Delaying his research will only delay the entry of Dslots. We must think about their complete eradication," said Eva.

Noah expected this question and so he explained, "Delay will give us breathing time and also time to initiate other tasks to erase GPRS completely. I will not mind if your task can even erase it." He paused, waited for any more query, and then Cooper interrupted, "But why Roger? He just joined Rotunda and is not aware of his powers."

Noah placed his hand on Rogers's shoulder and concluded, "You all are the chosen one. Sometimes powers are not needed if you have the power of knowledge. Be together and use each other's power to save Electon."

Research Of Cooper

They all walked out of Noah's cabin thoughtfully.

"As I have read so far, GPRS is based on frequency and time both, that is duplexing them together," Eva said promptly. Eva had a deep understanding of many concepts as she read and understood different technical updates happening in the human world. That's the reason she had been a part of many more tasks that had been initiated before to save Electon.

"But there is no source of frequency duplexing available with humans as of now. It's still in Electon," Cooper added.

"No, that's not correct," Eva said and stopped to pull a chalk from her pocket. She looked around to find a suitable place to write and then decided to use it on the floor. As she sat down, all others went on their knees.

"Using frequency means it's known as frequency division duplexing. This means that the transmitter and receiver operate at different frequencies." Eva drew a box and wrote Frequency Division Duplexing within it.

"I am not getting this," Olivia said, confused.

"I expected it," Cooper said peeved.

"Please stop Cooper, we need to work as a team,"

Eva said, looking at Cooper and started explaining to Olivia, "when humans make a call, they are transmitting signals to the other mobile which is called the receiver. In frequency division duplexing, both transmitter and receiver work on different frequencies."

"But then Cooper is correct, humans do not have this duplexing till now," Roger added, looking at Eva and added, "We made the first mobile call recently and it was on time division."

Eva looked wistful and then explained, "In initial days, where humans were in the signalling technology, they used Ham radios. That is, humans started developing mobile technology now but they have been transmitting signals and information for long. In old times, equipment was different and called with a different name, but with time, they got advanced and now reached a level of mobile devices."

"Oh! Shit! Shit! Man," Cooper said, pressing his hand in anger.

"What happened?" Olivia questioned, worried.

"Ham Radio was used in professionally wired telegraphy during the 19th century to mock operators with poor Morse code sending skills. In that, they send and receive Morse code both at different frequencies in a simple way that was duplexing of frequency."

"Morse code was used in telegraphs where dots and dashes were used to encode text messages as standardized sequences. How can that be said as duplexing?" Roger questioned.

"Can you please explain to me in detail?" added Olivia.

"In the old days, when a voice call had not been discovered, humans discovered a device called the telegraph. It used to send messages in the form of code.

These codes were in dots and dashes. This means to say for alphabet 'A', the code was one dot followed by one dash, and for alphabet 'B', the code was one dash followed by three dots. Similarly, each alphabet and number had a unique code." Cooper paused and looked at Olivia if she was getting it.

"Makes sense, please explain further," said Olivia.

"When any information was supposed to be sent, the telegraph was used to press dots and dashes as per the message, and on the receiving end, the operator noted these codes and then decoded them to attain the real message."

"Got it. And you want to say that different frequency was used at both ends?" replied Olivia after understanding the clarification.

"Exactly," said Roger.

"This might not be used but we must remember that humans are aware of duplexing, which is a must for GPRS. Our work must have been easy if they did not have that information, but now it's a big task for us," Eva added, overwrought.

"So, what next now?" Roger questioned.

"Eva, you study about Morse code and bring your findings. Olivia, you keep an eye on Bernhard. Roger and I will work on Samuel Morse," Cooper narrated the plan. This was the power of Cooper. He was quick in designing a plan.

"But why Samuel Morse?" Eva questioned and further added, "He was long past, and why do we not hit directly to Bernhard?"

"Sometimes, the past has answers and solutions. We may not be able to change the past but it can help us to modulate the present. Samuel Morse invented the telegraph and knowing more about him may help us in our task. We never know what could help us," Cooper added.

"Makes sense," added Roger.

As per the plan, they dispersed to work on their tasks.

"Let's move to the library to find out more about Morse code," said Eva to Olivia, as they both walked to the other side of the Arch.

On the other hand, Emma walked to the cabin of Noah after taking his permission.

"Tell me, Emma, how may I help you?"

Emma looked worried and then questioned, "Is it correct to involve Roger in such a big task, will he be safe? Anagol may be against that."

Noah took a step and started cleaning the mirror behind his desk and then said, "Sometimes what we see in the mirror is not exactly what we are. Similar is the story of this Electon. He is involved in this task as he is the only one who can stop shedding the blood of a Dslot in this task, else it will be tough," he explained on a serious note.

"But what about Noise; he can get to him on the task?"

"Noise can get any of us, it's we who need to be alert. If he fights today, he will live longer, Emma."

Emma had no other word. She nodded and moved out of the room after thanking him.

Eva and Olivia reached the athenaeum on the 300th floor of Rotunda. The athenaeum in Electon was massive, with millions of books and journals which were written by not only Vslots but also by humans. The athenaeum consisted of journals from thousands of years before Christ, some original documents could also be traced to have been written by people from the Maya civilization and even at the time of Ramayana. Every single word written in the human world had a copy of it added to the athenaeum.

The athenaeum was a massive room with extended shelves that had the height of approximately a hundred feet and covered the walls back to back; not a single glance of the wall could be seen. Vslots used this athenaeum for the task given to them and also to study their past and existence of Electon.

"How may I help you today, Eva?" said Sita, the document identity registrar of the athenaeum.

Sita was in charge of the document control of Electon. She was well-versed with each and every document present in the athenaeum by heart. She wore a sari and looked gorgeous with her long black hair. Her dark complexion was a cherry over a cake on her perfect figure and sharp features.

Sita had an Indian look as she was a Vslot who got developed as per the knowledge atom of S.R. Ranganathan. He was a mathematician and librarian from India and was well-known as the father of library sciences.

"We are looking for documents on Morse code, if you may suggest," Eva said with respect.

Sita listened, smiled, and then asked her to follow her. Sita walked to the farthest corner of the room and then entered details about the document on the screen placed on one of the shelves and pressed enter. One of the books which was placed on the topmost shelf came out on its own and reached Eva as it flew.

"You will get all technical specifications about the Morse code in this. Feel free to call me for any help," Sita said and walked back to her seat. Eva and Olivia moved fast and reached the backside and took a seat in silence. Eva started turning the pages read about all the details of the topic while Olivia closed her eyes and started concentrating on listening about Bernhard.

Olivia, being a humanoid of Bernhard, could get information about his thoughts and actions if she meditated. This technique was known as augur in Electon and was specially taught to Vslots who were humanoids. Olivia was still not an expert in that technique but she knew how to start augur.

On the other hand, Cooper and Roger reached the cottage areas of Arch Rotunda. The cottage area was behind the main building and was a group of abandoned cottages. These cottages were used for visitors in the past. It was said that in the history of Electon, people of Mars and Pluto visited Electon to build electromagnetic energy sources; these cottages were used by them.

"Samuel Finley Breese Morse was born in 1791 and died in 1872. He invented the Morse code and telegraph along with Charles Wheatstone after the death of his wife," Cooper explained to Roger.

"Who was Charles?" Roger questioned.

"Charles was an English inventor and scientist who invented Wheatstone bridge and also was a part of the development of the telegraph," Cooper explained.

"But then why should we think about Charles? We must find out more about Samuel Morse, as he was the inventor of the telegraph and Morse code," Roger added.

"Agreed, but Samuel was not a scientist. Although he invented Morse code and telegraph, he was basically a painter," Cooper said and paused to think, placing a pencil in his mouth and then said, "if this task were so simple to just stop Bernhard, Noah would not have involved four of us. There is something more which we need to find out."

"If we could have travelled time, we could have met Samuel and got our answers," Roger said casually.

Cooper listened to him and then replied excitedly, "You are correct, Roger. This is what is needed."

"What is needed?" Roger looked puzzled.

With a smile on his face, Cooper said, "Time travel."

With a peering expression on his face, Roger looked at Cooper. "Let's meet Eva and Olivia now. They must be in athenaeum. Let's go to them," Cooper said and started running fast, holding his book while being followed by Roger.

"But why do you always run, Cooper?" Roger said from behind.

They both reached the athenaeum and started searching for them. For Roger, the whole place was new, but still, he started enjoying life in Electon. He informed Cooper on their way, "Electon is interesting, I love it." And as usual, Cooper was not interested in what Roger was thinking. Cooper's eyes were moving fast in all directions as he was moving between the large bookshelves; sometimes, he stopped and looked back and sometimes looked from between the books, and then Roger said, "There they are, at last."

Cooper smiled and rushed to them, "Eva, I have a finding."

"We too have done some research; it's not as simple as it looks," Eva said, blinking her blue eyes while Olivia was still lost in her thoughts.

"You go first," Cooper said to Eva.

"Morse code was developed by Samuel Morse, we know that. But it was Charles Wheatstone who helped him," Eva took a pause, and Cooper added, "Yes, because Samuel was a painter and he was not a technical guy, but Charles was a well-known physicist and was already working in electromagnetic fields."

Eva nodded and continued, "Apart from that, Charles also made the Wheatstone bridge. I am not sure how but my inner feeling says that the Wheatstone bridge is somehow linked with this task."

Roger stood up from the chair and walked back to Eva, thinking, and then said thoughtfully, "If I remember Wheatstone bridge correctly, it's an electrical circuit that measures electrical resistance. In simple language, a balancing method to ensure that Noise must not enter the process."

"Exactly, you are correct in the human world. In Electon, it's something which is balanced by four legs to ensure that Noise must not enter Electon or affect Vslots," Cooper added.

"But what is that? And what does it have to do with this task?" Roger questioned thoughtfully.

"We can keep this question aside as Wheatstone bridge had been discovered many years before Electon was created; it may have relevance but not to that extent I feel," Cooper said and after a pause, he continued, "Eva, what Roger and I feel is that somehow, if we travel to the time of Samuel Morse, we may get some information which could be helpful to us. That information may help us to stop Bernhard."

Eva thought for a second and then said, "Maybe or maybe not, but there is no loss in trying it. We have three days in hand before the start of the task."

"It's a shadow of a girl, getting ready with a bundle of paper," Olivia said softly on the spur of the moment, still with closed eyes, lost in her dream.

All three of them immediately turned towards her to listen to what she was murmuring. They knew she was a humanoid of Bernhard and as she was trying to connect with him, she might spell out some critical information.

"What shadow, Olivia? Try to look clearly," Eva said, coming closer to her.

Olivia looked by stressing her mind which could be noticed as her eyeballs could be seen moving even when her eyes were closed. "She wants to share some vital information with Bernhard."

"Who is she? Can you see her?" Roger questioned.

Olivia further stressed and then replied with a pause, "No, it's not clear."

A drop of tear could be seen coming out from Olivia's eyes and she looked disturbed. Cooper asked Eva to wake her up else she could land up in complications. Eva immediately called her name to wake her up, but she was still in the human world. Eva then placed her hand on her shoulder to shake her.

Olivia opened her eyes, confused and in pain. "My head. It's aching."

"Do not worry, you will be fine in a few minutes," Eva replied, placing her hand on her forehead.

After waiting for a few minutes, Cooper questioned Olivia, "You were saying something about the shadow of a girl?"

Olivia looked dull, but she tried to recall and then replied, "I cannot see her face but she is travelling to Bernhard to share some important information."

Cooper asked if she could explain the information she was about to share.

"Not sure, but Bernhard received a telegram in which she said that she had some important research information which can help him in designing GPRS."

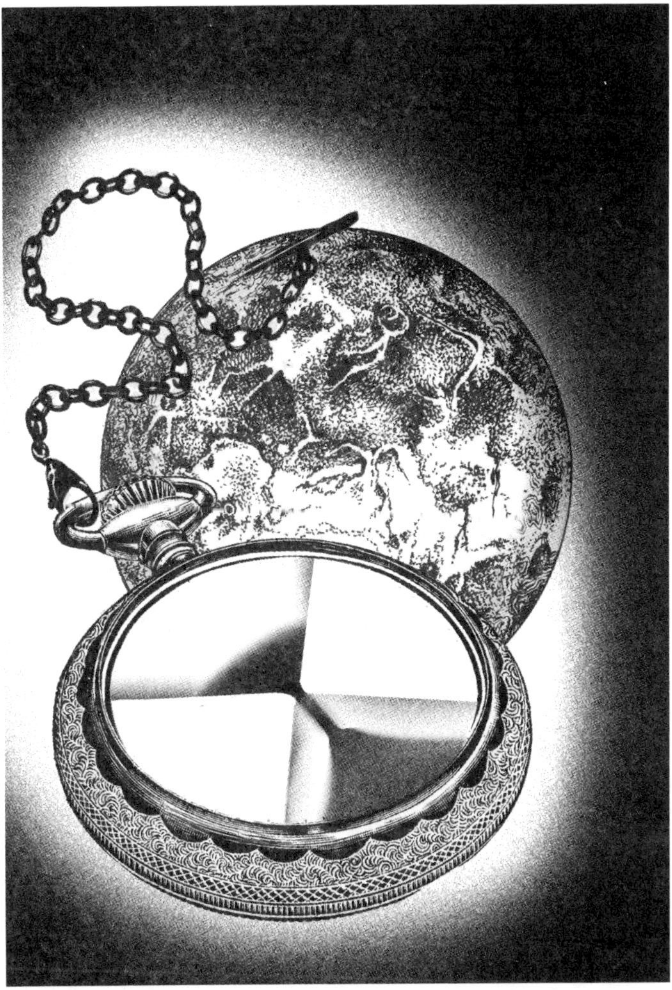

"It's quite possible that she may be his subordinate on this research?" Roger added.

"Maybe, but if that information is so important and if we can stop her, Bernhard may fail in his invention," Eva said.

They looked thoughtful, and then Cooper designed a plan of action.

"Roger and I will travel to 1825 to New York City to understand more about Samuel," Cooper explained, but before he concluded, Olivia questioned, "Why 1825?"

Eva had already read a lot and immediately replied, "Because Samuel got an idea about the telegraph at that time. Cooper, you are correct; that time would be best to know more details."

Cooper smiled and further added, "Eva, you need to study more and try to find out how Wheatstone bridge is linked to our task, and Olivia, you need to keep an eye on that girl whose shadow you saw."

They all agreed on the plan and stood in a circle to hold each other's hand to initiate the project. Roger smiled softly as he was happy to be a part of the team, but was also worried as he was still trying to figure out Electon. He had heard a lot about time travelling in the human world but never imagined that it could happen. He was assuming that they would get into a big machine in which he would set the time zone to travel in time.

"Let's move to collect our time travelling watch from Steven," said Cooper. Steven was responsible for checking on the visitors in Electon. He maintained the visitor update register in Arch Rotunda. He was a suspicious man as he suspected each one in the Arch, and why not! His responsibility was to ensure that no intruders must enter Arch Rotunda. He was known for the Polish dress which he wore. He wore the folk costume of Poland which consisted of a white embroidered shirt, a blue waistcoat (kaftan or vest) decorated with embroidery and tassels, striped or blue embroidered trousers, a hat called krakuska, a belt, and boots.

His nature was as colourful as his dresses, and he lived a lively life. He was too friendly with all the Vslots and always was ready to support them whenever he was needed.

He was busy in his cabin which was decorated with wall paintings and festival pictures from Poland. His desk was full of Polish Pisankis. They were painted eggs. The tradition of eggs painting goes back to ancient Mesopotamia, from where it spread to the region of the Mediterranean sea. The oldest painted eggs are of Sumerian origin and are about 5000 years old, and most of them can be seen decorated in his room.

"May we come in, sir?" said Cooper, knocking at the door.

"Oh! My dear Cooper, come inside," Steven said with a big gummy smile, and then he looked at Roger. He squeezed his lips and took a glance at him. He then placed his hands on his shoulders and kissed his forehead, closing his eyes.

"What a pleasant day that I met you, Roger," Steven said. Roger looked into his eyes and expressed his pleasure. While Cooper shared a request for the Venus clocks for time travelling, Roger was all astonished and pleased checking the baubles. In Electon, Venus clocks were used for time travel. These watches were round in shape, similar in size to the watches on Earth, made up of an element which was recovered from the volcano Maat Mon from the planet Venus and hung on a silver string. Among all the planets of the solar system, it's only Venus which rotates clockwise. Other all planets rotate anti-clockwise. This clock is synced with the rotation of the planet Venus to travel back in time.

"You look interested in the craftwork in my room, Roger," Steven said, giving a pleasant look, and then continued to search for keys in his drawer. "I was based in Poland for a task long back and the life there inspired me a lot. I loved the colours of life they used to keep to keep themselves happy and lively." Steven then removed one of the paintings placed just behind his desk. There was a keyhole in the wall. He started looking at the bunch of keys he was holding. A bunch which looked old and most of the keys in it were corroded.

"Ah! Finally, this is the one," Steven said, smiling, and then inserted the key in the hole. As he turned the key, a sound echoed in the room. Cooper and Roger looked inscrutable as the entire room started to move in the anti-clockwise direction, making them lose their balance. Roger immediately took hold of the desk and Cooper tried to grab the door to avoid falling while Steven laughed looking at both of them.

"Boys, do not worry; you will not fall overhead." The room kept on rotating. Soon, their bodies defied gravity as they hung upside down. But they didn't fall. To them, it looked as if previously they were inverted and now were standing in the correct direction.

"The beauty of Polish art is that they look the same from both angles," Steven added and started walking. He opened the door of his room from which Roger and Cooper entered. As they walked outside following Steven, they were perplexed as it was not the same Arch Rotunda but a big hollow room with space overhead. They could see meteorites and planets moving over them. The corner of that empty room had a wardrobe. A big wooden wardrobe, which was old but still looked new, with shining artifacts over it. Steven started walking to that wardrobe while they followed him. As they walked, Roger could see the planet Saturn moving above him. Roger was amused. Steven then opened the wardrobe. It had many shelves in it, with a number of Venus clocks arranged in there. He started looking among them and then picked out two clocks. "Cooper, will you mind holding the keys?"

Cooper immediately took hold of the bunch and

started walking behind Steven, who was still observing the Venus clocks. "We can travel in time with these small watches?" Roger questioned.

"Do not underestimate the power of this universe. It has many facts hidden within," Steven said and went back to the room. Cooper handed over the bunch of keys to him. He looked at the hole through his spectacles and then the room started to rotate back to its original position. This time, Cooper and Roger smiled at each other as they knew it would be a smooth landing.

"Hope you know how to use this, Cooper?" Steven questioned, handing over the Venus clocks.

"Definitely sir, you have taught us very well," Cooper replied and then turned to Roger. "Do not worry Roger, I will explain to you how to use this."

Cooper thanked Steven and was about to move out when Steven stopped them and walked closer to Roger. He reached close to his face and said, "Time-travelling could be simple but getting lost in time is the worst. Be safe and secure." Roger looked worried but nodded. Cooper assured Steven that he would take care of Roger. Once they both left, Steven closed the door of his cabin and then looked at the Pisankis in his room and picked one of the Pisankis and crushed it with his hands.

Portrait Of Lafayette

Cooper closed the door of their room and then turned to Roger. "First and most importantly, we must always carry the dust of Pluto with us," Cooper explained and showed the dust of Pluto which he had wrapped in a cloth, hanging by his waist.

"Yes, I too have this," Roger replied and pulled his wrapped dust from his pocket. Cooper explained that this bundle of dust must always be tied on his waist because if he encountered warriors of Noise, he would not have the time to search his pockets for the dust. Cooper helped Roger to hang it by his waist. "Whatever happens, this must be with you; it's your lifeline."

Cooper then pulled his Venus clock from his pocket to explain. That clock was not as simple as ordinary clocks were, it was different. It was tilted to 177° just like planet Venus. Inside that clock, there was a sand timer that was made up of the sand of Venus. Cooper explained that when they travel in time, they can only be at that time as per the sand timer. That time could be different for both of them. Once their time completes, they will automatically come back to the real-time and place, but if in between they want to return, they need to press the crown. Once the crown is pressed, it cannot be recalled, but by when will it take you back, it totally depends on the clock of Venus, which depends on the real movement of planet Venus.

"Isn't it too complicated?" Roger said with bug-eyes. "Really, is it?" Cooper gave a grave look, and then said, "Not to worry, do as I say and it's done."

Cooper further explained to him that the clock has three crowns; one is to set the year and the other two for day and month. Once that is established, they need to press each of the crowns. Once the last crown is pressed, they will travel in time.

"So when are we planning to travel? I am excited," said Roger.

Cooper looked pensive and then he moved to the cupboard placed on his side of the room. He opened its door to take out packets of chocolates and sandwiches and threw some of them towards Roger. "We must carry them cause what if we feel hungry."

Roger smiled and opened one chocolate immediately while Cooper turned to shut the window. The gong of the Arch started to echo marking the time to be seven in the evening. As Electon was always in darkness, it was the sound of this gong which made them aware of the time.

"Are you ready, Roger?" Cooper said with his brooding eyes. Roger nodded, giving a despondent look.

Cooper took hold of his clock in his right hand and asked Roger to do the same. Then they both set the first crown to 1825 and others to the first day of January. "We must press the crowns now," said Cooper, and they both pressed the first crown and then the second but before pressing the last crown, Roger interrupted, "But how do we know which city we need to travel to?" Cooper gave a chagrined look as he really forgot to tell that.

"Before pressing the last crown, you need to say the city's name followed by Lord Venus."

Roger tried to give a smart look and smiled. They both looked into each other's eyes with a grave look and then said together: 'Washington DC, Lord Venus' and pressed the third crown. They both closed their eyes, squeezing them tight because they were scared of flying in time. But everything was still as before. After a pause, Roger opened his one eye to check if really something happened, and then he opened the other one. He saw Cooper standing in front of him, glancing at him with his eyes wide open.

"It didn't work?" Roger asked, confused. They looked around and it was the same room in which they pressed the clock of Venus. "I think so too," Cooper replied with a haunted look on his face. But then they heard a sound outside their room.

"He is in the atrium, another side, come along." Hearing that voice, Copper moved to open the door silently and saw that outside was a completely different place. He turned and gestured to call Roger. Roger immediately moved to have a look.

"What is this place? We travelled in time?"

"Yes, come with me, let's check which place we are in," Cooper said, and they both walked outside. It was a passage with long carved pillars at equal distances, with a fire lamp placed on each one of them. It was very silent there.

"Should we not hide?" Roger questioned softly.

Cooper turned to him and then said, "They cannot see us, but yes, any action by us like the opening of the door or picking up anything can be observed. And yes, they can hear us too." By the time Cooper was explaining, an American lady in a black gown, with entirely made hair, middle-aged came walking towards them. Finding her coming towards them, Roger got scared and rushed back to the same room from where he had entered the passage and was surprised to see that the room was not the same anymore. Cooper tried to stop him but Roger did that too quickly to pay any heed to Cooper. As Roger turned, he saw that lady standing precisely in front of him looking there. Finding Roger in that position, Cooper placed his finger on his lips asking Roger to be quiet. Roger stopped breathing at that moment.

"How come this door opened on its own?" the lady said, turning towards the room. She stepped inside, checked the room, and then moved away shutting it back. Roger then breathed again. "I told you to be with me and listen to my instructions." Cooper scolded Roger in a gravelly voice.

"I am sorry."

"Now follow me, let us check the atrium," Cooper said to Roger, and they both started moving slowly. That place looked like a palace or some official building. One side of the passage had pillars at equal distance, and on the other side, there were doors to the room, which spread after each interval. There were big paintings of the rulers of Washington and their supporters on the walls. Soon they crossed the passage and entered the atrium. It was a big space with no roof head and was surrounded by pillars making the space circular. The fire lamp was placed on each of the pillars which were the primary source of light.

At the centre of the atrium stood Marquis de Lafayette, known only as Lafayette, who was a French aristocrat and military officer who fought in the American Revolutionary War commanding American troops in several battles, including the Siege of Yorktown. He was one of the dominant officials of that time. In front of him sat a man with a drawing board sketching his portrait.

He was a young man, tall and thin, with short hair. His fingers were moving perfectly on the drawing chart and his eyes showed with how much concentration he was painting Lafayette. He was Samuel Morse, who was known as one of the best painters of that time. He was specially invited to draw a sketch of Lafayette from his home town, New Haven, as his art was perfect and had no match. He wanted to finish that painting soon as he had left his wife alone at home who was expecting their third child anytime.

"Why don't you check the letter that the horseman delivered to you," Lafayette said, still standing in his fixed pose.

Samuel was lost in the sketch that he was making, and then after a pause, he said, "Sure, sir, just let me complete the final touch to your eyebrows."

Meanwhile, Roger reached behind Samuel and was amazed to see him. He had always studied in the human world about Morse code, and that day, standing next to him was exciting. Cooper was guiding Roger from behind to stay away from Samuel and not let them feel his presence. Samuel continued to draw for a few more minutes and then stood up from his seat after taking permission from Lafayette. "It's better; I can also use the washroom in this break," Lafayette said, stretching himself as he was tired of standing in the same pose for a long time.

Samuel placed his pen back on the table and walked a little to relax. He picked up the roll of cloth on which the letter was written by his father. As he read the letter, his eyes had an expression of shock. "Hope all is fine, Samuel?" Lafayette said, re-entering the room.

"My lord, the letter is written by my father stating the health condition of my wife. She is not well in her last days of pregnancy."

"So you want to leave the work," Lafayette said and added, "I think you must visit her."

Samuel looked confused and then, after thinking for a while, replied, "Sir, I am thinking to inform them that I will leave from here the day after tomorrow. By that time, a major portion of the sketch will be done." Lafayette had no objection to it. Samuel wrote a reply stating his plan and asked the horseman to take it back to his father.

Cooper took hold of Roger and pulled him into another room. He checked if it was empty and that no one could hear them, and then he said, "Roger, we can run time faster so that we can get what we want."

"Can we move time?" Roger questioned.

"If we can travel in time, we can play with it too."

Cooper then explained to him the use of the fourth crown by which they can fast forward the time in which they were. "If this clock I can carry into the human world, then I would know who would be my girlfriend in future," Roger said, smiling.

"But, you are just ten years old here," Cooper replied with a sarcastic smile.

As explained by Cooper, they fast-forwarded time and reached the third day, when the horseman was back again with another letter. This time it devastated Samuel as it stated that he lost his wife while she was giving birth to his third child. They tried a lot to save her but could only keep the boy who was healthy after birth.

Samuel started packing his stuff on finishing to read the letter. Lafayette was supportive and made arrangements for him to reach his home quickly. Samuel was lost and in pain. He loved his wife a lot and was in agony of not getting the message on time.

Samuel boarded the carriage which was arranged by Lafayette for him. Lafayette specially asked his servants to ensure Samuel reaches on time. Samuel's eyes were filled with tears as he moved to his home town. He knew he might not be able to see the last rites of his beloved as he would take another three days to reach. He regretted not starting his journey on the same day when he received his father's letter. He cursed mankind and the distances on Earth because of which communication took a long time.

Cooper and Roger decided to fast forward time to another three days and visit the hometown of Samuel. They were not exactly sure on which day he got the idea about the telegraph and so they were moving in time to know the details without losing time. When they moved in time to after three days, they saw Samuel in deep pain because when he reached after three days, her body had been buried and Samuel could not even see her face for one last time.

Cooper and Roger were sitting next to Samuel in his small house in New Haven. It was night and the only light came from the fire lamp placed at the corner. Samuel had not eaten for two days and had been crying on his fate. Cooper pulled a sandwich from his pocket and offered one to Roger. "We require this, I know," Cooper whispered in Roger's ears.

Roger took one and continued looking at him. He was feeling the pain of Samuel and could understand how difficult life was without technology. Somewhere in his heart, he felt proud of Electon and him being a Vslot. After waiting for a while, he pushed the sandwich to Samuel's side slowly, who was sitting there with his eyes closed which were full of tears.

"What are you doing? Once left by your hand, it will become visible," Cooper whispered again to Roger, but Roger knew what he was doing. He ignored Cooper and waited for a reaction from Samuel. After a few minutes, Samuel opened his eyes and wiped them. As he placed his hand to his side, he touched the sandwich placed there. He turned back and looked astonished to find it there. He looked surprised as he knew no one had come into his room. He looked at it with curious eyes and then picked it up. He then looked up, remembering his wife and with wet eyes, said, "I know you are communicating with me in your way." He paused, took a bite, and then continued, "Why are we humans so helpless when we want to communicate. I promise, my love, this distance will become shorter." He wiped his tears, saying, "I am not sure how but I will do it."

Cooper and Roger moved out of the room. "I have read that Samuel shared his idea with Charles Wheatstone on a ship in which he was travelling to go back to complete the sketch of Lafayette. I think we should move to that time and check what they discussed, it might help us."

"Agreed. Charles was the one who developed an electric telegraph later," Roger said and continued, "but now I am in doubt, what will we gain by knowing the information about all this?"

Cooper thought for a while before replying, "Bernhard is developing GPRS, and for that, he must know that it's possible only by frequency duplexing. Frequency duplexing was first used in the telegraph. If somehow we can fail his invention, it may not reach further to Bernhard."

Roger gave a quizzical look and then said, "But that will change the entirety of history."

"That is exactly what we want. If we change the past, the future will automatically adjust to the past, adjusting the memory of each and every individual," Cooper replied.

"But that means, there would be no Morse code, no telegraph, don't you think it would impact a lot?"

"It's not like that, we would only erase the frequency duplexing part from his research, not his complete invention. He would still invent the telegraph but by different methods."

"And what would be that method?" Roger further questioned.

Cooper smiled, "Our task is to stop Bernhard. Noah would then think and assign a new task to help Samuel. He will let us know the method to be suggested to him. A method which would be in favour of Vslots."

Roger thought for a second and then said, "Which means whatever technology evolution happens in the human world is as per Electon?" Roger turned back, thought more, and then added, "We made the first mobile call; it was all because Electon wanted it. But why? If that had been stopped, there would be no voice calls and no hungry humans for data. Everything would be perfect."

Cooper turned to him placing his hand on his shoulder, "No. Development in human world technology happens as per the increase in the population of Vslots in Electon. If Vslots are not engaged, they will start using the energy source to a greater extent, resulting in the drying off of the energy pool which will cause the end of Electon." Cooper further added, "Electon wants to take the human world to a higher level of technology but only with Vslots."

Roger turned back to him and looked in his eyes

to say, "And what about humans, did anyone ask them what they want?"

"We are just warriors. Let the Queen of Electon decide what needs to be done," Cooper said and then further explained to him that they need to travel to the time when Samuel met Charles. They set the time to after eight days and pushed the crown to reach the ship, which was sailing in darkness with fifty crew members and travellers.

The ship measured in tonnes of ancient rusting metal, was painted grey and black, and was peeling and blistering like a lousy sunburned. It had a noisy engine that was rattling and had cutlery jittering across dinner plates. Below the puff of grey smoke stood Samuel, lost in his own thoughts. The water beneath the ship looked angry as it was roaring and forming white bubbles. The water let the boat jump over the water like a toy.

"Thoughts can get better with a cigar," said a man to Samuel from behind. Samuel, who was busy in his thoughts and was looking at the roaring sea turned.

"Hello, I am Charles Wheatstone, and if I am not wrong, you are the famous painter, Samuel Morse?"

"You are correct," said Samuel and picked one cigar from the pack Charles offered. That was a small gesture and a conversation began for the most significant invention of the human world–the telegraph.

"I am not sure how famous I am but I know my pain is at its peak," Samuel replied, with a grave look.

Charles lit a cigar for him and with a pause, said, "Hope everything is fine, gentleman?"

Samuel turned towards the sea and then replied with a brittle voice, "I lost my wife."

Charles immediately said sorry for his loss.

"I loved her a lot and she understood every thought of mine, even those I never told her. When I felt hungry, she would bring food to me without me saying it to her; if I was not well, she knew it by looking at my face; she knew when I was in tension and held my hand," Samuel said and then continued with a pause, "communication needs to be as quick as we read emotions, else we will keep regretting by losing smiles over time."

Samuel shared his grief of losing his wife and about the idea of wanting to build something that can cause communication to be much faster.

"In ancient times, in China, messages were sent by drum beats, by making a typical sound for each alphabet. That sound varied in sound and strength," Morse explained, and continued, "I have something to show which may help you to guide me as you are a physicist." Samuel pulled out a piece of paper from his pocket. To look at that paper, Roger and Cooper also stepped towards them. That paper had alphabets written over it and against each alphabet, there were dot and dash combinations drawn.

"What is this exactly?" questioned Charles.

"Despite making a drum noise, I used something to demonstrate each alphabet in a dot and dash form. Now the only challenge is how to transmit these codes to another end?" Samuel said, taking a puff of his cigar. Charles knew he was having a discussion which could be very useful for human evolution and so he started showing interest. He stood up from his seat and walked to the corner of the boat, took a few puffs thinking, and then turned to say, "Last year, one of my research colleagues, William Sturgeon, invented the electromagnet."

"What is an electromagnet?" Samuel looked curious.

"Simply, it's a magnet which is powered by electric current," Charles replied, and then continued, "with the help of that electric, current can flow from one end to another via wires."

Samuel now stood up from his place and reached near him, "But how will it solve my problem?"

Charles said, "If somehow your dots and dashes can transmit over that wire," he paused and then continued, "codes can be transmitted from one end and the other end can receive the code and then decode it."

"Huh, but how to do that?" Samuel questioned.

"If I would tell you that, I would be inventing it." He laughed, paused, and then continued, "I would have joined you but I am busy with my research. But yes, I can guide you for sure." Charles took a few more puffs to say further, "You need to think what device you need to create; when it comes to the transmission, I can guide you."

Samuel thanked him and then further questioned, "If this communication runs on the wire, only one message can be delivered at a time or do we need to create a web of wires for each user?"

Charles thought for a while and then said, "In ancient China, if the receiver was near, they used a drum in a low tone and if it was far, they used higher sound. That means the frequency of the drum varies. I am not sure how, but you need to work on using the concept of frequency as used by China."

"And this is what is frequency duplexing, the main idea that was given to Samuel by Charles," whispered Cooper to Roger. Cooper gestured Roger to come along and they both walked to the other empty side of the ship.

The other side of the ship had a lot of fish gathered in baskets which had been captured by sailors. Cooper placed a handkerchief over his nose to avoid the smell. "Samuel was not a technical person and its sure that Charles helped him with his study. Should we travel further in time and understand what information he shared?" Roger said to Cooper.

'I think you are correct, Roger. Let's fast forward to one month later."

They looked around and started setting the time in their Venus clocks. "Let's move," said Cooper, and they pressed the crown. But this time, something different happened. Roger landed as if he had been thrown away in time. He found himself lying on his back in the foyer of Queen Anagol. It was dark out there, with minimal light from the fire lamps. Roger could not see things clearly and then he realized that his spectacles were lying to his side, which fell during that travel. He picked them up and looked to the side from where he could hear a girl speaking. He placed them over his eyes and turned to check the sound.

He could see a girl standing in front of the massive closed door of Hertzonia, busy shifting the colourful blocks and whispering Avalonia. Roger could see her golden hair open till her shoulders from the back. She was moving her hands fast over the blocks. A loud noise could be heard as those blocks moved places.

"How come I reached Hertzonia?" Roger said in a low voice. Listening to him, that girl turned, while those blocks were still shifting their positions. Roger was surprised to see Eva standing in front of him with a cheesy smile on her face.

"Welcome, Roger. You made my work easy," Eva said, taking a step towards him. Roger took the support of his hands to stand and said, "What work, Eva? And how did I come here? I must be with Cooper."

Eva came near him and let her hand move softly over Roger's cheeks, "I came to welcome Bumblebee for you, and look, you already came for him."

Roger looked at her with a puzzled look and then questioned, "Who is he?"

She walked to his side, and with a laugh, she replied, "Oh my God! You do not know Bumblebee? Your mother didn't teach you much."

Roger turned towards her to question and understand when those blocks suddenly started moving quickly, making a terrific sound. Roger and Eva both turned to look at the door which began to open. A cold wind with snowflakes started entering the foyer of Hertzonia as the door started to open. Roger turned his face and covered it with his hand while Eva started laughing loudly, letting all her golden hair fly and snow deposit on her face. Her voice grew stronger and stronger as the door opened wide. Roger looked from between his fingers to know the intruder and was surprised to see a giant man standing in front of the door.

He was huge; about twenty feet approximately, with elephantine muscles all over his body. He was just wearing shorts to hide his vitals and was scratching his body thoroughly as if he had not taken a bath for decades. His presence was stinking Hertzonia and he seemed to be yellow in colour in the light of the fire lamp. His body was full of thorns, small and big. He entered Hertzonia and looked all around as if he was searching for something with his big eyes. Roger noticed that he had no eyelashes. His nose was wet and dirty and he had unbrushed teeth. Finding him inside, Eva clapped her hands and shouted, "Welcome, Bumblebee! Welcome to Electon."

Listening to her, Bumblebee looked down at her and then at Roger and then drooped. Finding him bending down, Eva moved back with a faint smile on her face and rushed to hide behind the pillars while Roger was confused as to what to do. Before Roger could have decided anything, Bumblebee turned towards him and brought his face very close to Roger. Roger was afraid but stood facing him and avoided any movement. Bumblebee looked at him and roared, his saliva was flowing down his mouth. Roger felt like vomiting because of his smell but decided to be still. Bumblebee then came closer and tried to smell Roger with his grubby nose, and then said, "Son of the Queen. The task was so simple, my lord." He then stood again, making a lot of noise while scratching his stomach, and then he raised his hands to crush Roger, saying, "Time for Electon to witness…" Before Roger could understand what the giant was up to, Bumblebee brought down his hands rapidly to smash Roger on his head. But then, right before impact, Roger dissipated, spreading into pixels. Bumblebee's hand smashed the floor, breaking it to pieces while Eva covered her face with her hands to save herself from the bouncing particles.

"Where have you been, Roger? I was so worried," said Cooper as Roger reached back to him in the time of Samuel.

Roger looked muddled, finding himself back with Cooper and looked around.

"What happened, Roger?" Cooper said and placed his hand over his shoulder. "When you didn't reach along with me, I got afraid and immediately applied the search option in the Venus clock. Somehow it worked and brought you back."

Roger anxiously said to Cooper, "I am not sure what happened but I reached the Hertzonia entrance." He paused and then continued to explain, "We need to rush back to the real-time, something serious is happening out there."

"What happened? Who did you meet? We need to get the information from Charles," Cooper added, trying to understand the situation.

Roger looked into his eyes and then questioned, "Who is Bumblebee?"

Hearing the name Cooper went silent, and then with a grave look questioned, "Did you see him?"

"Yes. He entered Hertzonia and was about to tell me his reason."

"It's impossible. He is a warrior of the devil Noise and he is the strongest," Cooper said with fearful eyes and then continued, "but he can never cross the frequency-controlled door of Hertzonia."

"Warrior of devil Noise?" Roger gave a quizzical look.

Cooper understood that he needs to explain to him, and so he did. "In the human world, a humming sound comes when you make a call or when one is silent. That sound in the human world is called Bumblebee, but if you understand, it is a type of noise or disturbance created by humans themselves to ensure that the call is connected."

"Yes, I know."

"But in Electon, as it's a type of disturbance, he is a part of the devil Noise. But he is so vast and massive that it is tough to kill him. If he entered Hertzonia, he definitely would be having a serious plan. We need to inform Noah urgently."

Cooper started setting the return details in the Venus clock, saying, "But I am not sure how he entered as that door only opens for Vslots."

"It was opened by a Vslot," Roger informed, feeling haunted.

"Have you seen him, Roger?" Cooper looked at Roger inscrutably. Roger then informed him about Eva opening the massive door of Hertzonia by chanting Avalonia. He also told him the happiness she had on her face.

"Eva can't do that. It's implausible," said Cooper but

had no choice than to trust Roger.

They had to go back quickly to the real-time. They both pressed the Venus clock crown, and within no time, they were back to their own room in Arch Rotunda. They looked around to ensure they were back and then Cooper opened the door and saw many Vslots running on the corridor of the floor. All looked tensed and worried, and then they heard an announcement which was running on the intercom: "All Vslots must be in their rooms. We have an intruder in Arch Rotunda. You will be informed when things are normal. Till then, be safe in your places. In all rooms, Pluto dust shield is activated."

The message was loud and clear to all. Roger and Cooper understood who the intruder was. Arch Rotunda had an emergency facility of activating the Pluto dust shield which kept warriors of devil Noise away.

"What's the shield all about?" Roger questioned.

"It's the shield of the same dust that we carry with us, but it's on a large scale. It takes up a lot of energy of the frequency pool, so it is used only in an emergency situation."

Roger opened the door again and peeked outside. He looked at both sides and then turned back, "We must go to Noah."

"But it's not safe outside, we must wait for the next orders." Cooper wanted to follow the rules, but Roger had a different plan. "Noah must know that it's Eva, else she may create more problems if not informed on time." Before Cooper could have replied or agreed to him, Roger opened the door and ran outside.

"Wait, Roger," Cooper shouted but then rushed behind him, making an expression of a pained face. Roger decided to take the stairs to move to the lower floors. The stairs were wide with long steps constructed of wood. As they ran, the floor creaked loudly due to their footsteps. After reaching three levels down, Roger heard someone outside the door which opened towards the corridor.

"Wait, someone is here," Roger informed Cooper, who was behind him. Roger safely reached the door and tried to open it a little to know who was there. It was Greg standing in front of Emma. They both looked worried and were trying to figure out the situation.

"He is stuck in the telegraph room," he said to Emma.

Emma looked tensed and then she said, "I am not sure till when we can stick him there. The dust of Pluto will go out of stock soon, and he would become furious by then."

He looked thoughtful and then questioned, "When is Noah reaching?"

"He is on his way, he went to Mount Spuder."

"Can't he use his Venus clock?" Greg said.

"His Venus clock has stopped working and Steven cannot be found to fix it."

After a further conversation, he and Emma decided to reach the telegraph room which was behind the abandoned cottages. They chose to be at a safe distance as Arch Guards were on their duty.

"Is Venus clock with others also?" Roger turned, closing the door and questioning Cooper. Cooper confirmed to him that Venus clock is used permanently only by Noah, else it's issued by Steven when there is a requirement.

"Bumblebee was about to say something to me when I ran out in time." Roger looked thoughtful and then continued, "Eva can only reach Hertzonia gate without the help of Ber if she has a Venus clock, but as per you, it's not with everyone."

"So you want to say, it was someone else and not Eva?" Cooper questioned.

Roger had no words but his eyes spoke a lot, and then he said, "We have time in our hand, we can stop him."

"That would be a suicide attempt, Roger," Cooper said peeved.

Roger looked sure regarding what he wanted to do. "I am travelling to Hertzonia to the time before Bumblebee entered."

"That would be wrong, Roger. I am not joining you."

Cooper rejected his plan, but Roger was unstoppable as he had made up his mind. He pressed the crown of Venus clock and vanished, leaving Cooper standing alone. "Shit, man. Roger is a fool." Cooper thought for a second biting his nails and then pressed his crown, setting a time in it.

Time For Bumblebee

Roger travelled in time and found himself on the stairs a few hours back. Everything was normal. Vslots could be heard laughing and chatting. He pulled open the door and walked outside. Everything was normal as usual. Before going to the time when Bumblebee entered, he wanted to ensure where Eva was. He started walking towards the elevator as he tried to reach the athenaeum where he had left Eva and Olivia. As someone else entered the elevator, he joined them. As he was travelling in time, he could not be seen by anyone else. Soon he crossed the corridor and reached the entrance of athenaeum. He saw Eva coming out with Olivia. He reached closer to them to learn what they were up to.

"You need to focus Olivia and know who is she," Eva said to Olivia.

"Yes, Eva. I doubt that she has the information about frequency duplexing, which is carried to Bernhard." Olivia looked tired.

"You take some rest in your room; meanwhile, I will meet Steven to learn about Wheatstone Bridge in Arch," Eva said and started moving towards the cabin of Steven.

As per Roger, she might have taken the help of Steven to travel time and reach Hertzonia. Steven was the only one responsible for Venus clocks, and she might have ditched him with his gadgets. Roger decided to follow her.

She crossed the corridor, holding a book about the telegraph in her hand. She looked calm and steady as she walked. Her facial expression had no evidence of a big plan. She reached outside the cabin of Steven and knocked at the door. "Hello, my dear Eva, pleasant to see you," Steven said as he opened the door.

"Sir, I have a few questions, I hope you won't mind helping me with them?" Eva said politely. Steven happily welcomed her inside his cabin. Roger took advantage of the gap and entered along with her and stood to a side. "Let's discuss over a cup of tea. I was about to have one." Steven offered her a cup of tea and then asked her about her doubt.

"Sir, I am on a task," Eva started, but Steven added before she concluded, "Along with Cooper and the son of the Queen."

"Exactly!" she replied and added, "I read journals in athenaeum and came to know that Samuel Morse got help from Charles Wheatstone for his invention about the telegraph. But Charles was busy inventing Wheatstone bridge at the time when he supported him. I feel that Wheatstone bridge has something to do in this task."

Eva was not sure if Wheatstone bridge was linked or not, but she did not want to leave any stone unturned to make the task a success.

"Do you know what is Wheatstone bridge in the human world?" Steven questioned before giving a reply.

"It's an electrical bridge with four legs. Balancing of

those legs helps one to know the electrical resistance."

"Perfect, my child," Steven said, smiling and then added, "think about those four legs in Arch Rotunda which are always balanced and they create a balanced image. It only disrupts when warriors of Noise enter the bridge."

Eva started thinking, what structure in Arch Rotunda resembled it. "Take a sip of the tea; it will help you recall," Steven said, offering her tea again. Eva smiled and took a sip. Steven continued to look at her with a peering look and then she started yarning. Soon her beautiful blue eyes started blinking as she found it tough to stay awake. Within no time, she dropped the cup to the floor and slept. Steven continued to observe her and then said, "Silly girl. Have you not seen the court of Queen Anagol with four pillars creating the same image of her each time."

Roger now understood what connection was of Wheatstone bridge with Bumblebee. The court of Anagol had four pillars and each of them was connected by lines; when Anagol comes to the room, she appeared in four different points. As those four pillars were balanced as in Wheatstone bridge, they worked as a force to stop warriors of Noise from crossing the court. But as Eva opened the gate of Hertzonia, that bridge was broken and Bumblebee entered Arch Rotunda. Everything was clear to Roger, but he was still doubtful what was the role of Steven in all of that. Why did he make Eva fall asleep?

Steven then shifted the Pisanki of his room to enter the room where Venus clocks were placed. He picked up Eva in his arms and put her in the room between the clocks.

"Sorry, Eva, but someone needs to be sacrificed for the change," Steven said while picking up the Venus clock. Roger now understood that it was not Eva but Steven, who opened the door for Bumblebee. Roger had to reach the foyer before him so that he could stop Steven before Bumblebee came.

Roger was about to press the crown when one of the photo frames placed on the side table fell on its own. Roger turned but then decided to leave and rush in time.

Roger decided to rush, and so he adjusted his Venus clock and pressed the crown to reach before Steven to the gate of Hertzonia. It was dark and silent. The Wheatstone pillars stood guarding the foyer. Roger looked at each side to ensure that he was all alone and then hid behind one of the pillars. He remained silent, controlling his breath, waiting for Steven to enter, but then he realized something. As he was travelling in time, he would be invisible.

After a few minutes, he saw pixels flying in the air. Those pixels were of multiple colours and sizes, not more than a particle of dust. He observed them flying and when they reached the centre, they tried to accumulate to form Eva. Roger was expecting Steven but looked quizzical, finding Eva again. Steven had done something to present Eva in his place.

Roger hid behind the pillar to observe what she was up to. Eva then looked around and walked towards the gate of Hertzonia. He could see her from behind, standing in front of the massive door, trying to move the rectangular blocks with her hands. And then he heard another sound of the pixels flying. Roger turned to check the intruder and was surprised to find another version of his own self lying on the floor. He could see himself observing Eva, who was busy shifting the colourful blocks and whispering Avalonia.

She was moving her hands fast over the blocks and

a loud noise could be heard as those blocks began to move places.

"How come I reached Hertzonia?" Roger said in a low voice. Listening to him, Eva turned while those blocks were still shifting their position. Roger was surprised to see Eva standing in front of him with a cheesy smile on her face.

Roger knew what was going to happen next and he was waiting for the right moment as he hid behind the pillar.

"Welcome, Roger. You made my work easy," Eva said, taking a step towards him. Roger took the support of his hands to stand and said, "What work, Eva? And how did I come here? I must be with Cooper."

This time Roger moved away from the pillar and moved to the door of Hertzonia and whispered Avalonia to change the blocks which he knew were set by Eva so that Bumblebee could enter.

Eva came near old Roger and let her hand move softly over his cheeks, "I came to welcome Bumblebee for you and look, you already came for him."

Old Roger looked at her with a puzzled look and then questioned, "Who is he?"

She walked to his side, and with a laugh, she replied, "Oh my God! You do not know Bumblebee? Your mother didn't teach you much."

Old Roger turned towards her to question when those blocks suddenly started moving fast, making a terrific sound. Old Roger and Eva both turned to look at the door which began to open. A cold wind with snowflakes started entering the foyer of Hertzonia as the door started to open. Old Roger turned his face and covered it with his hand while Eva started laughing loudly, letting all her golden hair fly and snow deposit on her face. Her voice grew stronger and stronger as the door opened wide. Old Roger looked from between his fingers to know the intruder.

Roger, on the other hand, had failed as his spell didn't work and the door was about to open. Eva was laughing while waiting for Bumblebee to enter but she went silent as the door started closing again. Roger understood that his pronunciation worked.

"It's not possible, he needs to come," said Eva and rushed towards the door to open it again. She looked peeved and dangerous as she again started to move the blocks. But this time, old Roger took a step and tried to stop her by holding her mouth from behind. He knew she must not spell Avalonia. Eva was struggling to free herself with one of her hands while moving the blocks with the other, but Roger, who could not be seen, was moving the blocks to the original position. Eva understood something was not correct and she pushed old Roger with her left leg. She again started to move the blocks while old Roger still kept trying to stop her. But this time, she turned towards him and pushed him hard, making him fly in the air to bump on one of the pillars. "You are too disturbing, Roger," Eva said, taking a step towards him, and then she moved her hand to her pocket and brought out sand. She then threw it over him, saying Avalonia. Roger could not understand what she did, but he saw old Roger feeling sleepy and fainting on the floor. She then turned back to the door while Roger rushed to check on old Roger and wake him up.

"Roger, you need to wake up," Roger said to his old self. While he was trying to wake him, Eva moved the blocks and pronounced Avalonia. The loud sound was enough for Roger to get distracted and understand that the door was again opening. He stood up and tried to pull the dust of Pluto from his bundle to throw over Bumblebee but doubted if such a small quantity of dust would work on such a huge monster. The door opened and Bumblebee entered.

He was huge; about twenty feet approximately, with elephantine muscles all over his body. He was just wearing shorts to hide his vitals and was scratching his body thoroughly as if he had not taken a bath for decades. His presence was stinking Hertzonia and he seemed to be yellow in colour in the light of the fire lamp. His body was full of thorns, small and big. He entered Hertzonia and looked all around as if he was searching for something with his big eyes. Roger noticed that he had no eyelashes. His nose was wet and dirty and he had unbrushed teeth. Finding him inside, Eva clapped her hands and shouted, "Welcome, Bumblebee! Welcome to Electon."

Listening to her, Bumblebee looked down at her, and then towards old Roger who was lying unconscious on the floor and then drooped. Finding him bending down, Eva moved back with a faint smile on her face and rushed to hide behind the pillars while Roger was confused as to what to do. Before Roger could have decided anything, Bumblebee turned towards old Roger and brought his face very close to Roger who was lying on the floor. Bumblebee looked at him and roared. His saliva was flowing down his mouth. Roger felt like vomiting because of his smell but was trying to decide his plan of action. Bumblebee then came closer and tried to smell old Roger with his grubby nose, and then said, "Son of the Queen. The task was so simple, my lord." He then stood up again, making a lot of noise while scratching his stomach, and then raised his hands to crush Roger, who was lying unconscious, saying, "Time for Electon to witness the death of Vslot for which Noise has been waiting for years. Now the time has come for the end of the regime of Anagol." Roger knew that Bumblebee was about to thrash him and so he took an instant decision and rushed to himself on the floor, and before Bumblebee could have crushed him, Roger pressed the crown of old Roger's Venus clock. Bumblebee's hands floundered on the floor, breaking the floor into pieces.

"Where did he go?" shouted Bumblebee and turned to look around. He was moving his heavy body all around, crushing the floor in the process. He drooped back towards Eva who was still hiding behind the pillar. As she saw Bumblebee's face near her face, she pleaded, turning her face to another side as she leaned on the wall.

"You didn't follow orders correctly, no need of you further," Bumblebee said softly and then took hold of her by her neck. Eva started screeching as her throat was getting chocked. Roger was not sure what to do. He thought that at least some part of the dust of Pluto may work. He immediately unwrapped his bundle of the dust and threw it high over Bumblebee so that it spread all over his body. But he was surprised as the quantity of the dust was much larger then what he had in his fist. He turned around, finding Noah along with Cooper spreading the dust of Pluto all over Bumblebee. Roger looked at them, smiled and nodded a thankyou. All three of them circled Bumblebee. He shouted and roared in pain, throwing Eva to the other side. Eva was thrashed to the wall and fell unconscious.

Due to the dust of Pluto, holes on the body of Bumblebee could be seen becoming large with blood all over. He shook and got unsteady. He turned to check the source of the dust but could not find anyone there. He shouted and tried to run away, opening the main door and pushing it with both his hands. As he ran outside, Hertzonia shook as if a quake had occurred. He tried to but could not escape and fell on the snow-covered ground. He closed his eyes in pain as he was going to meet death. His saliva covered his face.

Noah turned as the red lady warriors reached the spot. "She needs to be taken to Quodtophet and interrogated."

The red warriors bowed to take the order and placed a glass bottle with a cork cap next to Eva. Then they put their hands over the other and murmured something. Roger continued looking with curiosity as Eva began to disperse into pixels and entered the bottle. A single drop of tear could be seen in the eyes of Roger and Cooper as the bottle got filled with her pixels. One of the red warriors then closed the jar with a cap and placed the bottle in a bag hanging by her waist. "Permission to leave, Noah?"

"Hun," Noah said and then turned to Roger. "Some confusion. I think it's Steven and not Eva who is the culprit." Roger tried to explain. Noah continued looking into his eyes and then said softly: Avalonia, and in the next moment, Roger was standing on the topmost point of the Rotunda along with Noah.

Roger turned to look around. He could only see dense green clouds all below him. The wind was blowing in the darkness of Electon as they stood at the top of Arch Rotunda, the mast. The mast was made up of yellow granite stone. Noah looked deep into the eyes of Roger as he explored the situation.

"What we believe sometimes can be equally enigmatic and can capture you in your own enigma," Noah said in his gruff voice.

Roger looked at him patiently as he continued,

"Roger, you must have waited for me to take action."

"I am sorry, sir, but that is what struck my mind at that moment."

"Some moments can be so crucial that they could have taken away your life and not only your life but the fate of Electon."

Roger listened carefully feeling downcast. Noah, after a pause, took a step towards him and then said, "Promise me, Roger; in the future, if you were in any such situation, you will alert me before deciding your action." Roger looked in his eyes and then nodded in agreement.

Noah, after giving him a curious look, turned and started moving back. He turned again and said in a low voice without a smile, "But always appreciate your action and your thought process."

A sudden smile appeared on Roger's face. But he had more questions for which he needed answers, and so he said, "But sir, why Eva?"

On hearing his question, Noah looked at the clouds to answer, "She was a Vslot, no doubt in that. But somehow she was inspired by the Dslot Oryut whom she met a year back on one of her missions. She started believing in the fantasy of Oryut but she kept her feelings hidden. She started supporting Dslots."

"But Bumblebee was not a Dslot; he was a warrior of the devil Noise, right?"

"Yes, this is what still needs to be explored; why Bumblebee and not a Dslot," Noah said. "When she read the journal about Wheatstone bridge in the athenaeum, she understood that it could be a pathway for warriors of Noise if cracked. She knew that Steven was a good source of information and so she approached him. Steven, as expected, explained to her about Wheatstone bridge but he also offered her the tea of truth."

"Tea of truth?" Roger questioned.

"It's a tea which will put you to sleep if you are questioned something for different reasons as mentioned, and Steven understood it as she started feeling sleepy. Steven did a perfect job by taking her to a separate room to get more information about her intentions, but he was not aware that she had already taken an antidote. She woke up in between and sprinkled the sleeping dust on him. She then took the clock of Venus to reach Hertzonia without the help of Ber."

"I am still not clear how Steven could understand all of this by just the sipping of tea?" Roger interrupted.

Noah calmly explained, "The tea of truth is made up of tea leaves mixed with the bones of a dragon, grilled by the fire of the dragon. The fire of a dragon is the purest form of fire which is generated by the inner depth of the dragon and not by any external source." Noah paused and then continued, "Anyone who demands something but is not saying the truth will fall asleep after having it, as his inner truth does not match with the facial truth. The same happened with Eva."

"But how do you know all of this?"

"She didn't have sufficient encrypted codes with her to kill Steven so she could only make him sleep. In Electon, one who has more encrypted codes is more potent than others." Noah paused and then placed his hands on Roger to continue, "Steven, when woke up, understood that she might have ditched him as one of the clocks was missing. He travelled in time to meet me and handed over the new clock to me."

"It's not Cooper who called you?"

Noah continued staring at him before saying, "Say thanks to your friend who came to help you unconditionally."

Everything looked confusing to Roger, as he could not believe that Eva could design such a big conspiracy to let Bumblebee enter. He didn't inform Noah about his time travel to Steven's room because he left before Eva applied sleeping dust on Steven and hence, did not know everything. He regretted leaving early from that time. He even thought to travel back again and investigate whether what Steven has communicated is correct or not, but going back again meant changing history again and Noah warned him to not take any action without his permission. Also, he was worried about what if something wrong happened this time and Bumblebee took over Electon.

Future Strategy

Plenty of blue and white pixels could be seen flying over the Googleplex in the future of Electon. The Googleplex is the corporate headquarter of Google in Mountain View, California, United States. If Arch Rotunda in the real-time was the house of Vslots, in the future, Googleplex was the same for Dslots.

Googleplex was covered in the darkness of Electon when those pixels started to combine to form Markboo. After Roger was taken away by the warriors of Anagol, Markboo decided to go to Googleplex to meet Googol.

Googol was the most complex and influential person among Dslots, whom humans called Google in their world. He is to have the most massive army of Dslots; if to be counted in numbers, his army size would be a digit one followed by a hundred zeroes. The world of Dslots was ruled by three significant rulers, Markboo, Googol, and Malus Pumila.

Markboo decided to meet them to plan their strategy because their previous strategy failed as Roger was not with them. It was his plan to bring Roger from the human world and use him as a Dslot to take over Electon before time, but apparently, their plan failed.

Googol was known for his generous nature and

designer clothes in the future of Electon. He was a handsome American man, tall, clean shaved with short brown hair, and every hour, his clothes changed on their own.

Markboo walked inside the vast campus of Googol. The castle of Googol was of relatively low height and sprawled over a large area of land. The interior of Googleplex was furnished with items like shade lamps and giant rubber balls. The lobby through which Markboo passed had a piano and a projection of algorithms running for different tasks Dslots were running through. Googol had designed a sophisticated algorithm to track each and every move a Dslot took to complete the project. Similar to Vslot's, they too design various tasks to take over Electon but they have an advanced methodology to keep track. Each Dslot was connected by a complex network of cosmic rays that sent signals to Googolplex based on the usage and interruptions of the cosmic environment of the Dslot in various time zones. These interruptions and variations in cosmic radiation were calculated by an algorithm and measured to know the progress of the task. Markboo then passed through a huge dinosaur structure to enter the significant courtroom.

"Welcome, Markboo!" said Googol, standing in front of him, dressed in a white attire. He smiled and continued, "We didn't expect you to fail."

Markboo smiled and took a seat in his own style and said, "Hope warriors of Dslot would have joined me."

"Hopefully, if we were informed about the action you were planning in advance," Googol replied, taking a seat.

"Some decisions need to be confidential."

Googol banged his hand on the table and continued speaking with his glowering eyes, "And because of your this decision, Roger is in Arch Rotunda. Our future is at stake."

Scornfully, Markboo looked at Googol, "The plan was to bring him in our team but they got the information."

"Because you forgot that Crawler is still with Anagol, informing her about each and every movement in Electon through his web network."

Crawler's network was powerful not only in Electon but also extended to the human world. Crawler had always been a communication source for Anagol and updated her about all the happenings in both the worlds. He was the one who suggested Anagol to hide Roger in the human world using the path of the bulb so that Roger could be protected from Noise.

Markboo was downcast as he knew he made a mistake. After a pause, Markboo questioned, "Now you suggest Googol, what should we do."

Googol stood up from his seat and looked thoughtful. He then said, "The time in which Roger is now functioning is of Vslots. They have all the opportunities to erase our existence, a small mistake we make can change the future of Electon." Googol paused and then continued, "As per my information, Vslots are about to stop Bernhard from his invention of GPRS which is the first step towards Dslots existence. My warriors are on task. She has been given all information about frequency duplexing which was shared by Charles to Samuel. She will take them to Bernhard."

"And who is she?" Markboo questioned with a confused look.

"Some decisions need to be confidential," Googol

repeated the same dialogue and smiled.

"If Bernhard succeeds, a path for Dslots will open up in Electon. Then only we can plan to weaken Anagol," Googol said.

"Don't you think Crawler would play his role?" Markboo questioned.

"I am the future, and I will write the future of Crawler," Googol said, raising his hands.

Room Of Alva

In the recent time of Electon, Roger, holding a book in his hands, was running towards the athenaeum in Rotunda. He looked at the entry gate and climbed the stairs to enter. He was searching for Cooper and Olivia. He knew they had lost time in their task and they need to rush to stop Charles from sending the information to Samuel. He started searching for them in each corner and then he heard whispers at the last corner of athenaeum. He stopped and peaked to have a look.

"Olivia, anything more you could know?" Cooper questioned Olivia. She was tired and looked lethargic.

"What happened?" Roger questioned on reaching them.

"She is trying hard, but the only information is about the girl assigned to deliver documents to Bernhard."

Roger, before replying anything, hugged Cooper and then said, "Thanks Cooper, for coming as my saviour." Cooper smiled and replied, "Anytime, friend."

"Should we travel back to the time of Charles Wheatstone?" Roger questioned.

Cooper looked depressed hearing that and then said, "That time has passed Roger. Charles delivered information about using different frequencies for transmitting and receiving signals to Samuel."

There is always a time gap between the past and the present time, and for any task, that gap needs to be maintained as every step runs on that fixed time gap. Cooper knew the concept of time gap and was able to easily calculate that that time was over in the past.

"And how do you know that?" Roger questioned.

Cooper knew he had to explain to him, and so he did, "Steven has a space bowl in which anything happening at the same time in the past can be seen."

Roger listened carefully and then replied, "Which means if I want to check what happened at this time in any particular year, it can be monitored?"

"Yes, that space bowl is connected internally by the web of Crawler, which keeps on feeding the information based on its algorithm. The water in the bowl reflects that image. The space bowl works on the phenomena of the time gap. Whenever we look in the space bowl, it will record your present time and then as per the time gap running in the Electon world, it will show you the past."

Roger thoughtfully said, "Can we have a look at that?"

Cooper suggested that they need to meet Steven who could show it to them again. On agreement, all three of them walked to Steven's cabin.

Steven opened the door and welcomed them. Roger requested Steven to show them the situation in which Samuel was at the moment in the past so that they could plan their move accordingly. "It's one of my duties to help you, Roger," Steven said and took them to the corner of his cabin. At the corner, he placed a glass bowl over a stand of glass. The water in that glass was crystal clear and stagnant. The bowl was made up of molten glass which was recovered from the 'blue marble' alien planet about sixty-three light-years from Earth. Blue marble planet was known for its molten glass ruins which happened because of the high temperature of its sun. As per journals in Electon, this glass was brought to the world of Electon by aliens who handed it over to people from ancient Egypt. Later, this was taken away by Vslots in the world of Electon. The water in the bowl was from the moon, which was collected at the beginning ofhuman civilization. It is said that the moon was full of several oceans and lakes at that time, with a beautiful, civilized life. It was noted that the Electon world existed on moon at that time, and this water was recovered from the ruins of the moon's Electon after Anagol took over the Electon of Earth. The Electon world of the moon was destroyed because soon after Dslots came up, mankind slowly finished themselves.

"Whatever time you need to check, you need to write it in a paper and place it in this bowl," explained Steven.

Suddenly, the door of the cabin opened. "Steven, are you coming along?" asked Greg, who went silent after looking at Roger, and continued softly, "Roger, the son of the Queen. Congratulations on your success." Greg said it sarcastically.

Roger looked at him and then replied to say thanks. Greg continued to look at him strangely and then said to Steven, "Will wait for you in the common room." But before he left, he softly pushed the broken egg art towards Roger, which was crushed by Steven earlier when he handed over the clock of Venus to Roger and Cooper. The egg touched his palm and so Roger looked into Greg's eyes which spoke a lot. Without further notification, Greg moved out of the cabin, leaving them with Steven. While Steven explained the space bowl, Roger thought about the meaning of Greg's action.

Roger picked up the paper and wrote the present time and date when Samuel was alive and dropped it in the bowl. "You need to wait for a second," Steven said.

Roger, Cooper, and Olivia stared at the bowl, waiting to see Samuel. After a few seconds, the stagnant water in the pot started creating waves and then an image began to appear in the bowl. They could see Samuel sitting on a chair next to a manufacturing table on which some electrical equipment could be seen. He was busy making some electrical connections with the copper wires. Next to the stuff was placed a paper on which alphabets were written and against them were written dots and dashes. Each symbol was different for each alphabet. "That is the Morse code," said Cooper.

"Yes, as he was a painter, he symbolized them in that way," added Roger.

"And only that, as his telegraph could be pressed once for a dot and long pressed for the dash, he symbolized them in such a way," Steven tried to explain.

"But if he was designing the equipment, he must already be having the knowledge of frequency duplexing for which we were searching," Roger added.

Listening to him, Cooper wrote something on the paper and dropped it in the bowl again. "What did you do?" questioned Steven.

"I want to check if that logic had been delivered to him by Charles."

Cooper wrote a date about ten days before. The stagnant water again started to move and what they saw was Samuel reading some documents written with blue ink. They understood that they missed the time when they must have been with Samuel to not let those documents reach him.

"We missed that time," said Olivia.

The water went back to a stagnant state and became crystal clear. Roger turned to Cooper, "What's next, Cooper?"

"I am not sure but before deciding anything, we must check what was in that document. We can get a copy from the athenaeum as every text created in the human world gets replicated in there. We cannot change it or stop it now, but at least know the information to decide what to do further."

"Cooper is correct, you must check that and let me know for any help," added Steven, smiling. They thanked Steven and moved towards the athenaeum. On the way, Roger, who was still confused with the gesture of Greg, questioned Cooper, "What could be the reason for crushed Pisanki?"

Cooper was not aware of it and he asked Roger to concentrate on the task, but Roger was under the impression that something was related to Pisanki which may help them. "You both continue to go to the athenaeum, I will join you in some time," said Roger and turned to move in another direction.

Olivia tried to stop him but Cooper stopped her by saying, "Let him check, he may be correct."

Roger decided to meet Greg and moved towards his cabin. His cabin was on the other side and he took the corridor to reach there. He was about to knock at his door when he heard someone talking. He didn't want to but decided to eavesdrop as he could hear his name.

"This could be dangerous for our existence," Greg said.

"And you are preaching this to me? You know what we are up to," another person said.

"I am only concerned about the son of the Queen, rest is your matter." Greg paused and then continued in his crocky voice, "Do not excite me to commit a mistake."

A laugh was enough to help Roger understand that the other person was Steven, and then he said, "Your decisions may affect Electon, so calm down Greg." While Roger was at the door trying to listen, the latch of the door was pushed, making a sound.

"Shhhh…" Greg placed a finger on his lips to alert Steven. Greg then took a long step and pulled the door to open it and saw Roger standing outside. He looked at Roger with suspicion and then questioned in his hard voice, "Do you need something, Roger?"

Slack-jawed, Roger was surprised and then tried to manipulate, "Ah…actually, I wanted to know something from you." Although Roger wanted to ask about the crushed Pisanki from Greg, he changed the topic.

"And what's it all about?" Greg asked, showing him his earnest eyes.

Roger thoughtfully replied, "I want to know what is Quodtophet?"

Steven came out of the room and smiled at Roger, saying, "Roger, I thought you would be in the athenaeum."

"Ya, I was supposed to but had some query," Roger replied while Greg continued looking at him with suspicion. Steven stood aside and continued to look at Roger with a smile; he preferred to be a part of their conversation.

"Quod means prison and tophet implies hell. It's the prison of Electon which is worse than hell. The culprits are taken in there and kept in glass bottles and those bottles are heated until they regret their fault,"

Greg explained.

Roger paused and then thanked him while looking at both of them. He didn't want to ask about Pisanki in front of Steven and he thought it would be better to have a word with Emma. Somewhere in his heart, he still felt sad for Eva. He doubted the effigy of Steven but he had to be sure. He excused himself from Greg and then turned to walk towards the cabin of Emma. While he was on his way, he saw Emma at the other end of the corridor, getting some notice placed on the notice board with the help of Elfo. Elfo was a short boy, who worked as a caretaker in the Arch. Roger took long steps to walk towards Emma.

"Excuse me, Emma, is it the right time to talk to you?" Roger said from behind her. She was surprised at hearing the voice and turned with a polite look and said, "Yes, Roger, we can."

Roger looked at Elfo and gave a look through which Emma understood that he needs some privacy. She took hold of Roger by his shoulder and directed him to a side, asking Elfo to continue with the work. After reaching behind a pillar, she looked into his eyes for his query.

"What is Pisanki?"

"That's all?" Emma gave a strange look and then continued, "It's an egg art of Poland."

"That's in the human world. What is Pisanki in Electon?"

Emma looked to both sides and said, "Pisanki is used for time travel as they vary in colours that help to create pixels to cross the boundaries of time."

Roger continued looking in her eyes and then said, "What is the meaning of crushed Pisanki?"

"Crushed Pisanki could happen when you want

someone to get lost in time or make him reach some different time and place where he or she is not meant to be." She paused and then questioned, "Have you seen a crushed Pisanki, Roger?"

Roger was silent for a while and then replied, "No, not at all. It was just a query."

He thanked her and was about to turn to go back to the atheneum when Emma said, "Roger, Electon is the world where who is a friend and who is your enemy is the toughest part to judge. Be safe and be alert always." Roger looked at her and then nodded.

On his way, he could now understand why he reached Hertzonia while he had time travelled to Samuel. Maybe because of the crushed Pisanki which had been done by Steven. But then why Eva was in Quodtophet. Is it possible that Steven used Eva or they both were together in this conspiracy? If they both were involved, then Steven must also get arrested, and if Eva is innocent, she must be freed.

Anyhow, the first task for him was to stop Bernhard, and for that, he now had to meet Cooper and decide the next action plan. He rushed to the atheneum to meet them, but then he saw Cooper and Olivia coming towards him.

"Roger, Olivia has seen that girl. We have very little time left," said Cooper, reaching to him with chagrined expressions. Roger turned to Olivia, and she then said, "Roger, she is one of the telecom employees in the human world and is doing her research since long on frequency duplexing. She had cracked the concept of frequency reuse in the telegraph. When she heard about Bernhard in one of the seminars, she decided to contact him and share with him her thesis. She already flew from Finland to Germany to meet him."

"Then it's time for us to enter the human world and stop her. What's her name and how will we find her?" Roger questioned Olivia.

Olivia stressed her mind with closed eyes, and then said, "She is an employee of Telenokia in Finland." Olivia paused while Roger added, "I worked there, I know each one of them. Tell me the name."

"Olivia, you can do it," added Cooper, motivating her.

With a pause, Olivia replied, "Milla. Her name is Milla–a young, dynamic, and beautiful Finnish girl."

Roger took a step back, gave a grave look, and then he said thoughtfully, "She never informed me about her research."

"You know her, Roger?" Cooper questioned, placing his hand over his shoulder.

"She is one of my very close friends. I can ask her directly to not share that information with Bernhard."

"Wow! So our task just got so simple," added Olivia.

Cooper was still musing in his own way, and then he added, "No, we must not talk to her directly."

"Why? She is one of my best friends. She would understand."

"But what if she got followed by Dslots or warriors of Noise, who want Bernhard to complete his invention. Her life could be in danger then."

Roger looked concerned about Milla on hearing the point raised by Cooper. Olivia supported Cooper as he continued, "Roger, you need to be with her and try if those research papers can be taken away without her knowledge. I am sure Dslots will be there to hinder our way, we need to be extra careful to save her."

Roger looked at Cooper to say, "I am thankful that you show concern for her. I agree we need to complete the task without any harm done to her." Roger paused and then added, "So what's next?"

"We need to go to the Alva room from where we can travel to the human world," Cooper said.

"Alva room? Can't we use Venus clock for the same?" Roger questioned.

"No, we are not travelling in time now but going to the human world in real-time. We need to enter the human world using the bulb made by Thomas Alva Edison," Olivia explained in her fruity voice.

Cooper knew all this was new to Roger, so he started to explain to him on their way to the Alva room. He said that Alva room was specially designed on the three hundredth floor of Arch Rotunda for enabling Vslots to travel to the human world. It's the room that has the original bulb which was invented by Thomas Alva Edison. It was the first gateway of Electon to the human world, and since ages, Vslots have been using it. Roger listened to him and questioned, "How come Markboo came to the human world when Arch Rotunda is only for Vslots?"

Roger had a valid question as he had met Markboo in his world sometime back. Cooper further explained to him that as Dslots are in the future, they exist in Arch Rotunda; that's the main reason Vslots were fighting to stop and change their future. Cooper also explained that entering the human world could be done only via the Alva bulb, but returning could be done by either bulb, telephones, or mobile phones to the world of Electon.

"Which means Markboo used Alva bulb in the future of Electon to reach the human world?" Roger questioned to confirm.

"Exactly."

They then took the elevator to reach the floor of

Alva room. It was a magnificent floor. As the elevator door opened, they entered the corridor which was lit by fire lamps in the shape of bulbs at equal distances. Roger's eyes were on the wall which had huge painted pictures of Thomas Alva Edison since his childhood days. "I have never seen his childhood pictures," said Roger fascinated. Cooper explained that it's the only place where his childhood days can be seen as the human world has none of them. That floor depicted the complete story of Thomas inventing the bulb and all his contributions in the human world of technology. Roger stopped at one of the pictures and admired the beauty of it, which showed Thomas sitting in the lap of his mother who was showing him water in a bucket.

"We remember the inventor, forgetting that the thought was brought to him by his mother." Cooper nodded from behind, admiring the picture along with them. While Cooper and Roger were busy admiring the picture, Olivia walked to the corner of the glass window, and then said softly, "Cooper, come here."

Hearing her, Cooper and Roger walked to her. Olivia's eyes were stuck on something outside in the dark and then she fingered on something outside. Cooper and Roger took a glance and found something far on the other hilltop next to Arch Rotunda–a colossal castle was getting constructed in the darkness of Electon.

"All new technology development in the human world had a unique event in Electon. This is the castle of Bernhard, which will be completed for Dslots if we fail in our task," Cooper said sardonically. Roger took a step closer towards the window and had a look. He could see some dark shadows working at the site.

"Let's move, Cooper, we hardly have time in hand," Roger said to Cooper, taping him on his shoulder. They turned back in the silence of the Alva floor and walked straight to open the big front door. It was a massive door at the end of the corridor. Roger pushed the door open and they stepped inside. That room had an altogether different feeling. It looked as if they had entered into the ancient time of the human world. At the centre of the room, a round table was placed. It was a round table the size of a cartwheel made of rough wood. Around the circumference were rocks from every corner of the land set into the wood. Above that table was a bulb that was hanging and was antique in its own. It was a big bulb, coiled from the top, and was hanging on a wire. It was switched off but could be seen because of the light of the fire lamps in the room.

"It's the first bulb which got invented in the history of humans," said Cooper, looking at the bulb. Roger was amazed at finding it in front of him. That bulb tells the story of Electon in its own way. "We need to stand around the table in a circle," said Olivia. They took their positions at each corner and then Olivia raised her hand to hold Roger and Cooper with her hand. Soon, all three of them got ready to visit the human world holding their hands. "Together we need to chant Avalonia," said Olivia, and continued, "at the count of three."

Olivia then said one, Cooper with a pause said two, and then they both looked at Roger, who said three and then Avalonia. Their bodies started evaporating, getting divided into pixels, circling around the round table, and then, with a stream of light, they entered the bulb which had started to glow by then and as the last pixel entered the bulb, it again went off, leaving the Alva room back in the darkness of the Electon.

Back To The Human World

It was nine in the evening in Finland and the streets of the town at the Arctic Lapland were empty. In the darkness and silence, only bugs could be heard screaming to make the place seem lively. The street lights at equal intervals were trying to light up the road between the dark boundaries. The bugs were gathered all around the light to make a buzzing sound. The sky was clear and stars could be seen in the clear night sky. Suddenly, the bugs which were in thousands of numbers around the light started to buzz, flying all around the light and then rushed, leaving the light alone. After a few seconds, the bulb began to flicker and then with a loud sound, the light crashed out of the lamp, and Roger, Cooper, and Olivia jumped on the road.

"Welcome to the world of humans," said Roger and turned to smile at Cooper and Olivia, but was puzzled looking at the bug-eyes of Olivia, and then she said:

"I was not expecting you to be so handsome, Roger."

Hearing her, Roger realized that he was seeing Olivia and Cooper from a taller height. He immediately looked at his body and realized that he was back as

Rhythm in the human world as a twenty-five-year-old handsome boy.

"Are you having a crush on Roger?" Cooper said, teasing Olivia who was staring at Rhythm.

"Hopefully, as I now know that one day Roger will grow up to be Rhythm in Electon," Olivia replied, stunned. Rhythm tried to be humorous and instantly hugged Olivia saying, "Love you, kid." Cooper laughed and so did Olivia.

Rhythm then moved back and continued, "Listen, friends, we will move to my place and then we will call Milla to know what she is up to." Others agreed to his plan and they picked up a cab from a distance and reached his home. Rhythm tried to search for the keys that Uncle Gourd usually placed in the hideout behind the flower pots when the home door opened on its own.

"I am not only Uncle Gourd but your guard, Roger. Come in," Uncle Gourd said, opening the door, with a beer in his hand.

"You started again," said Rhythm and hugged him.

"This is what I love about humans–the beer," Uncle replied and shook hands with Cooper and Olivia. They walked inside following Uncle Gourd. "This reindeer meat still looks fresh," said Rhythm picking up a piece to bite.

"Why not, I cooked it this morning only."

Rhythm placed the piece back and with a strange look, said, "You cooked it when Markboo took me away; it's been very long now."

"It's long in the Electon world. In the human world, it's just a few hours," Uncle replied happily. Rhythm thoughtfully took a seat on the sofa next to Olivia and then said, which means Milla was working on frequency duplexing research since long but didn't inform me?"

"Should she inform you?"

"We shared everything. Why did she hide this from me?"

"Is she your girlfriend?" questioned Olivia. Hearing her, Rhythm gave her a pitiful look.

"Why don't you call her?" said Uncle, dropping a piece of bread that Concha took away immediately.

Rhythm decided to call Milla without talking about her research because they thought that it could land her in some trouble. Rhythm stood and picked up the landline phone and looked at Uncle Gourd, saying with a humiliated look, "Can you fix this line now, please?" To keep Rhythm safe, Uncle disconnected everything in the morning. "Oops! I'll do it right now." Uncle Gourd stood up from his place and reached the corner to fix the lines. "How much time it will take?" Rhythm asked, taking a seat.

"Just a second." Uncle chanted Avalonia and all the wires started moving on their own and got fixed within seconds. Rhythm gave a bleak look as he now understood how he managed to restrict the whole house in such a short duration. Rhythm picked up the receiver and dialled the number of Milla. After a few rings, her grandma picked up the call. She was old and Rhythm knew he had to speak loudly to help her hear. She informed Rhythm that Milla had some official work at Aachen University, Germany, and she took a flight just an hour back. "We missed her, she is on her way to Germany," informed Rhythm to Cooper. They looked at each other quizzically to understand what they must do. Milla would reach in another thirty hours to Germany and she had a lot of time in her hand if she wanted to do some work during the flight.

"Why don't Cooper and I enter the flight in which

she is and try to get the documents she is carrying while Rhythm can directly reach Germany?" Olivia said.

"And how would you do this?" Rhythm questioned.

"We are not humans, Rhythm," answered Cooper confidently.

They made a plan that Cooper and Milla would enter the flight directly via the bulbs installed in the restroom of the plane, and Rhythm would directly reach Germany along with Uncle Gourd. They wanted to take away her documents in such a way that it looked as if she lost them. They reached the first-floor room of Rhythm after he confirmed with Milla's grandma about her fight details. Cooper placed the bulb in the empty holder which was handed over to him by Uncle. "Olivia, all set to go?"

Olivia nodded and looked at Rhythm. "I will wait for you in Germany," confirmed Rhythm. Within no time, Cooper and Olivia evaporated into pixels and entered the bulb, leaving Rhythm all alone.

"Welcome on board, ma'am," said the air hostess to Milla, who boarded her flight. Milla thanked her and reached her seat, which was the middle seat in the centre of the plane. She placed her handbag on the upper space and took her seat, greeting the men sitting on both sides of her seat. Within a few minutes, the flight reached the runway and took off to Germany.

A man wearing a black suit and grey eyes was sitting in the restroom of the flight when the light of the bathroom started to flicker. He turned his face to look at that and then stood up to adjust the light. He pushed the bulb to tighten it. For a few seconds, the flickering stopped but then it started again. He took back his seat and then looked surprised as the brightness of the bulb began to increase on its own, and then Cooper jumped out from the bulb into that small restroom which was good enough only for a single person to adjust. "Hello, sorry for bothering," said Cooper, finding someone already in the washroom.

"You landed in the wrong place, Cooper," said that man, standing in front of Cooper. It is not sure who threw the first punch, but suddenly Cooper's fist was in his face while the man sunk his in Cooper's stomach. He was a Dslot from the army of Googol on his task to ensure Milla reaches Bernhard on time. Purple blood pooled in his mouth as Cooper gagged. They stumbled apart for a brief second to catch their breaths before diving back at each other, eyes narrowed in determination. Cooper's fist was attacking fast, so was his. Cooper dodged his fist and came up with his own; for a brief instant, his eyes widened before he managed to tilt his head back and slammed it on Cooper's. Stars burst in Cooper's vision, but he shook it off and threw a sloppy kick. The man turned back in the narrow escape and said, "You can't stop her, Cooper." Cooper only heard a faint sound. He tightened his fist and hit the face of the man one last time, and then took hold of his head to twist it anticlockwise which made him fall in the small space of the washroom.

Once he ensured that he was dead, Cooper adjusted his clothes, looked in the mirror, and opened the door. That man started evaporating and converting into pixels, and entered the bulb, leaving the washroom empty.

As Cooper stepped out of the washroom, another washroom door opened at the same time. It was Olivia in the other. She looked at Cooper strangely and started walking to take a seat at last. While they both walked, their eyes were at Milla, who was busy reading a book. Cooper took a seat to the side row of Milla and then tried to enquire about her belongings. His eyes scanned the closed upper cabins and could see a single black leather bag placed just above Milla. He then turned and looked at Olivia who was sitting behind him and blinked to confirm to her about the documents. After waiting for some time, the man sitting next to Milla on the aisle side, stood up to go to the washroom. Cooper took advantage of the situation and reached Milla by taking the empty seat. Milla was still busy reading the book. While Cooper was analyzing Milla, the eyes of the air hostess were on Cooper who seemed strange to her. But she was confused as she could not believe someone to enter the flight while it was in the air.

"You look like an avid reader to me," said Cooper, trying to start a conversation with Milla. Milla closed the book and turned to look at Cooper through her spectacles. She then smiled and said, "Yes, my dear kid. Do you also love to read?"

Cooper then realized he was just fourteen. "Yes, aunty. I love to read Nancy Drew."

"Good, reading is the best habit," Milla said and turned back to her book. Cooper wanted to discuss further, and so he said, "You know aunty, recently, I read that mobile phones have been invented in Finland, are you not proud of our country?"

Hearing him, Milla smiled and closed her book. "Yes, I am damn proud of that." She paused, smiled, looked at him, and then continued, "This small device which has been named as mobile will change the world in the future. Soon, a day will come when this world will be connected, where distance will not matter. Everyone will be close to each other."

"Yes, voice can reach from one person to another at any place," Cooper added.

Milla again smiled and then said, "Not only voice

but soon data, which means pictures and videos too will fly in the air."

Cooper kept on thinking and then said, "Don't you think that will create distances?"

"How? People will be more connected."

Cooper thoughtfully replied, "When a mother would like to meet her son, he would meet her virtually over mobile and she would miss a chance to hug him; a day will not be far when kids would play on mobiles and a playground would be merely used for pictures, when couples would kiss screens and lips would be dry, when voices will be lost and text will be another way to speak."

Milla looked in the eyes of Cooper strangely, and then asked curiously, "Who are you?"

Cooper took a pause and continued looking into her eyes and then said, "Do not go to Bernhard, Milla." Milla was astonished at his words but before she could say anything, the man returned from the washroom and said, placing his hand over Cooper's shoulder, "Time to leave, my dear." Cooper looked at him and then stood up from his seat while that man continued to stare at him. Cooper turned and then he noticed something strange. Every seat of the plane had a man sitting on it wearing the same black attire and only Milla was a female if they excluded Olivia. All of them were sitting straight and silent. Cooper understood that he was in trouble as all the men were none other than the warriors of Dslot Googol and were already in the flight to protect Milla. His mind quickly took a decision to take away Milla's bag and evaporate into Electon.

Cooper turned back and pushed the man standing in front of him, letting him fall in the passage and quickly opened the upper cabin to pull Milla's bag. "Olivia, time to rush," Cooper shouted. Milla understood something was strange and she yelled to stop him from taking away her bag. Then a man sitting next to Milla took hold of Cooper's hand and twisted it causing Cooper pain; at that time, Olivia entered and gave a strong punch to his face, "Do not underestimate me, Dslot."

The Dslots stood from their seats; they had done this hundred of times, and this time, they were sure they have got the Vslots all alone. As the Dslot started to reach them, Olivia turned her face in the opposite direction to Cooper. In the blink of an eye, Olivia's palm snapped and the nose of the man next to her exploded and bled. Her leg kicked him with the force of a wrecking ball and made the man who was approaching her fly, causing others behind him to fall. Cooper then took the support of the back of Olivia and twisted his body to kick the man approaching him hard on his chest. They had to be quick as Dslots were many, they could not hold them for long. Cooper threw the bag towards Olivia, and two men took hold of Olivia's hand, trying to snatch the bag from her. Olivia first pulled the bag and when they tried to shoot, she left the bag and jumped to kick them while flying in the air, making them let go of the bag again.

Meanwhile, Cooper was not giving any chance to Dslots. He took a position in the aisle stopping all the other men who were trying to come forward, but there were many trying to jump over the seats to reach Olivia who now had the bag. Milla was afraid and took shelter between the seats. Air hostesses were also a part of Dslots and ready to fight.

Cooper turned to check Olivia when a man from behind kicked him on his back. Cooper lost control and fell on the ground. Another man jumped over him, facing his elbow. Cooper's face got cut, making his purple blood flow. Olivia was still holding the bag and was busy kicking anyone who was coming close to her. Cooper rushed to her and their backs faced the gate of the flight while they continued kicking and punching the men coming towards them. By then, almost all the men gathered in front of them and started knocking Cooper and Olivia. At that time, one of the men snatched the bag from Olivia. She tried to reach out, pushing the men in front, but then the door of the flight opened and Cooper, along with Olivia and few of the men, were pulled out of the flight due to the air pressure. Milla stood on the side, holding the handle to open the gate in confidence. The plane started to disbalance as the wind started entering with full force; everyone inside got suctioned towards the entrance. Milla took hold of the seat tightly to stay inside. The remaining Dslots on the plane grabbed some or the other thing to save themselves from getting sucked. Milla was afraid and was yelling for help. Soon, one of the Dslot took the initiative of holding each other's hand and one by one, built a chain. Finally, the one near to the gate managed to close it, letting everyone feel relaxed.

On the other hand, Cooper and Olivia were falling and reaching fast towards the ground without a parachute. "Do not worry, Olivia. Let me think," Cooper shouted to Olivia, who was near him and was afraid of falling down. Their hair and clothes were blowing in the air as they were falling at high speed. "We will die, Cooper," Olivia shouted.

"No, we will not. We have to live," Cooper shouted and then turned his body so that he could see down. Cooper could now see something on the ground. "Olivia," he shouted, but she looked depressed and closed her eyes in fear. He shouted her name again. This time she replied.

"I can see a lamp-post down there. Keep saying Avalonia, we might get suctioned inside there," Cooper shouted and started saying Avalonia. She also did the same in hopes to be saved. As they did not plan any place to visit, they were not sure where they would land after entering the bulb, but getting saved was more important then. They continued chanting the word while they were falling. It was hardly twenty meters when they crossed the lamp post. They both closed their eyes realizing that they were gonna hit the ground. But then, at the last moment, came flying the guards of Cooper and Olivia. In Electon, each Vslot had a guard just like Uncle Gourd for Roger. These guards usually did not interfere in the task but tried their best to save the Vslots, other than while they were in combat. They took hold of Cooper and Olivia and safely landed on the ground.

"Thanks a lot for saving us," said Cooper to the guards. They both were massive and robustly built.

"It's our duty, Vslots," they both said and vanished in the air again.

Olivia could not believe that she was safe. She was shivering in fear and had tears in her eyes. "We are perfectly fine, Olivia. Just relax now," said Cooper, trying to calm her.

Olivia could not speak for some more time and went on her knees to relax. Cooper waited for her to relax and when Olivia said, "I never desired to die without marrying," Cooper understood she was fine then.

Markboo Again

In Arch Rotunda, Emma had a peculiar observation since Roger informed her about the crushed Pisanki. She was suspicious of everyone. The only one whom she could trust was Noah. Emma was walking fast, taking long steps on the corridor of the Alva room as she knew that Noah was on that floor. She walked, holding a big book in her hand, which she read to find out the truth about the crushed Pisanki. She looked around and took quick steps and found him standing at the open gallery monitoring the new construction of Dslots in Electon. The golden-brown hair of Noah was moving in the wind on that dark night as he looked tensed and worried.

"Mr. Noah, you look worried," said Emma from behind him. Noah, who was unblinkingly looking at the shadows, replied while turning towards her, "Some failures make us realize how dependent we are on each other."

Emma listened and then said, "But we did not fail, Mr. Noah."

This time Noah turned and looked at her with pained eyes and then said, "Thousands of years ago, Electon world existed on planet Mars, the same way as it's on Earth now. The humans on Mars wanted all the luxuries of life and so they invented gadgets." He paused and then continued, "Those gadgets were used for calling, then pictures, and then those gadgets took over their brains."

Noah turned back to look at the construction and then continued gasping, "I have seen similar constructions on the Electon world of Mars thousands of years back. I have seen the human race end on Mars. This fight is not between Vslots and Dslots, but it's an attempt to save mankind because of whom we exist."

Listening to him, Emma looked at the book that she was holding and then said, "Since this space is created, the same story is repeating on different planets, and to our bad luck, the end is always the same." She paused. "The end of the human world. We have been trying since ages to save them and will keep on trying unless this space decides that humans have no place on any planet of this entire universe."

Noah again turned to her and questioned why she wanted to meet him urgently. She informed him about the crushed Pisanki which Roger asked her about. "I knew Pisanki could be only seen at Steven's cabin." She visited Steven's cabin to ensure that Roger had not seen crushed Pisanki in there when Steven was not in his place. Although she could not find a crushed Pisanki, she could notice the empty space where Pisanki had been placed previously. "I could not trace Steven anywhere in the Arch, I doubt if we are correct."

Noah looked thoughtful and then said, "Hun, I can understand your concern." He looked outside at the construction again and then continued, "Let's travel in time again." Noah explained to Emma that if her doubt is correct, they could know something by travelling in time when Eva met Steven in his cabin. "Before travelling in time, should we not visit Steven's cabin and check where is he using the molten glass bowl?"

Noah liked the idea and they walked to his cabin. Emma knocked at the door and waited, then realized that it was locked. Noah took a step back to say Avalonia and the door opened on its own. But to their surprise, the molten glass bowl was missing from its place. "I think your words have a solid reason, Emma."

In the human world, Rhythm decided to travel to Aachen, Germany as planned. "It's time to go, Uncle," said Rhythm to Uncle Gourd, who was busy having the leftover reindeer. Rhythm moved to his room and stood below the bulb placed in his room. This was the first time when he was travelling all alone. "Be safe and secure, Rhythm," Uncle Gourd shouted from the ground floor. Rhythm looked at the bulb with a brooding expression on his face, took a deep breath and then said 'Avalonia'. He soon realized that his body started to evaporate into pixels and started entering the bulb. Within no time, he found himself in the lonely bay of Aachen, Germany. He could hear the sound of the train. He adjusted the overcoat he was wearing and then ensured to read the poster on the wall. He took long steps to walk to the other side and saw people walking upstairs, taking the stairs. He immediately understood that he was in the subway. He followed the mob who just got down from the train and walked with them outside.

It was a pleasant afternoon in the town and he could see many people all around. He soon entered the major hub of the city. He walked on the footpath, observing the beauty of the town. He knew it was time for Milla's flight to reach and so he decided to have some snacks by then. He looked around and saw a coffee shop. He moved his hand into his pocket as he was worried that he was not carrying the currency of the city but then he tried something crazy. He said Avalonia and was surprised to find his pocket full of local money. He also ensured that his other pocket carried the sand of Pluto for his safety.

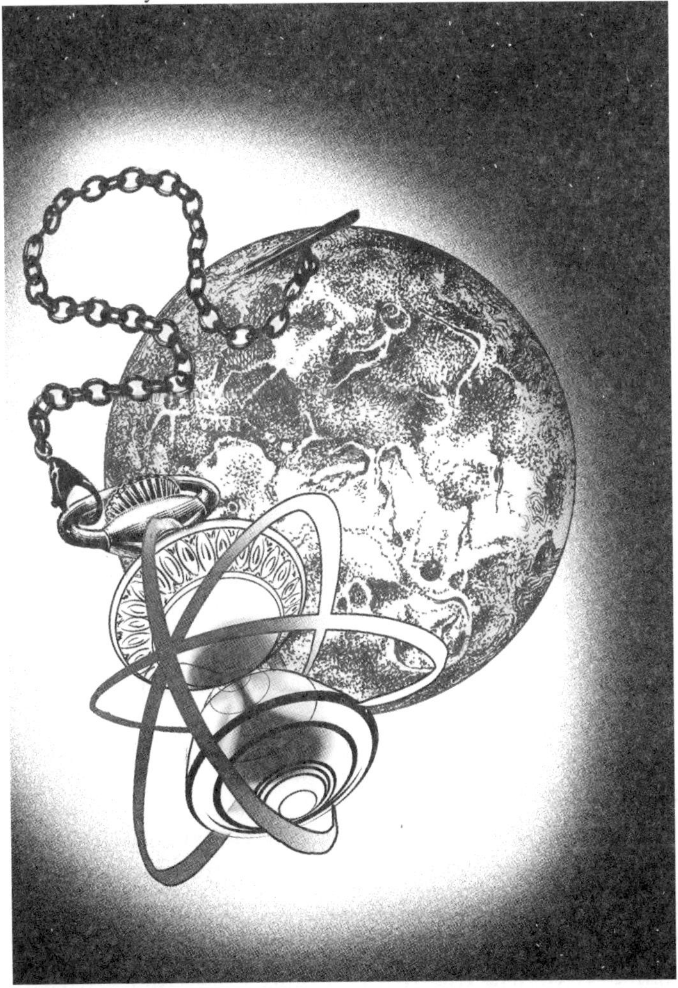

He walked inside and ordered a chicken hamburger and a cup of cappuccino. He always loved this combination. He took a seat in the corner next to the glass door. His eyes were looking outside, observing the locals dancing and playing music while he was waiting for his order.

"Good evening, Rhythm!" Rhythm turned in surprise on hearing his name and was further in shock and fear finding Markboo standing in front of him.

"You didn't miss me? I missed you a lot. May I take a seat along with you?" Markboo said, but before Rhythm could answer, he pulled the chair to take a seat. Rhythm waited for him to continue, reaching for his pockets for the sand of Pluto.

Markboo looked blithe as he looked to the other side and then smiled to say, "Rhythm, I forgot to tell you, this sand works only on Noise and not on slots." Rhythm looked puzzled. Markboo then pulled his chair and moved closer to him, made eye contact and said, "What will happen if you die tonight?" Markboo took a pause and then continued, "You are the only slot among Vslots and Dslots who has the resistance power against Noise. Because of you, the frequency pool is running. I am your friend and not against Vslots."

Rhythm now leaned back and looked outside before saying, "Markboo, can you see those dancing kids outside?"

Markboo looked at them and then nodded in agreement.

"They are dancing today and enjoying with their friends because you are not with them. In the future, when you will enter their lives, it will be ruined. They will only meet friends over the internet; they will only dance virtually. The world would be virtual with no feelings but just clicks to like and unlike." Rhythm paused and turned towards him, looking deep into his eyes, and said, "The world would become a slave of

Dslots and I am not going to let it happen." Rhythm gave a confident look to Markboo.

"What if I finish Vslots?" Markboo said sarcastically.

"And why do you think you can do that?" said Uncle Gourd from behind. Markboo turned and found Gourd standing to hold a chicken hamburger in his hand. "Sorry, Rhythm. I wanted to have some food so I thought to try German cuisine," Uncle Gourd said and took a seat next to Markboo.

"We can discuss the entire day on this topic, but you know, since ages, Vslots could not stop Dslots," said Markboo, looking at Gourd.

"And that's the reason many planets are now the graves of humankind," added Rhythm.

Markboo now stood up from his seat, wore his black goggles and said, "My job was to warn you." He started moving and then from some distance, he again turned to say, "Sorry to say this but your friends could not stop Milla."

Rhythm continued observing him as he left the coffee shop. "Uncle, are Cooper and Olivia safe?"

Uncle Gourd took a bite and then replied, "Yes, they are. Had a crash landing somewhere near the border of Berlin, but safe. My job is to eat this hamburger, you may continue with your task." Rhythm looked outside again, thoughtfully, but looked surprised, seeing Markboo dancing with the kids.

"It's time for me to reach the airport, Milla will be arriving anytime now," said Rhythm.

On the other hand, Cooper and Olivia were standing on the barren land somewhere on the border of Berlin. To the extreme end, they could see only barren land with stones and orange sand. "We had no option than to walk, Olivia," said Cooper, looking all around. As he looked above, he could see vultures flying in the clear sky. It was extremely hot.

"At some distance, you saw a lamp post, should we try to travel by that?" suggested Olivia.

"Better idea, we must walk to that side."

They started walking. Cooper was fast and energetic while Olivia looked tired. "Don't you think being human is so exciting?" questioned Olivia, walking behind him.

"Maybe, hope you like to fool yourself," replied Cooper, without looking at her.

"What do you mean by that?"

"We are fighting in Electon with Dslots to save the human world and these fools are celebrating the success of creating a world with them in it, without knowing the danger they are landing themselves into."

Olivia listened carefully and then replied, "It's because they are not aware of that."

Cooper was too intelligent to answer her, and so he replied calmly, still looking for a solution, "You must read the journals of the future. In the future, these humans would know how dangerous these Dslots are, but still, they do not leave it. This is because of their poor will power that many planets vanished, including Mars."

Olivia continued walking without replying, but she looked thoughtful. After walking a little more, Cooper hid his forehead from the sunlight and then shouted, "Olivia, we have a way out. We reached the lamp post."

"Thank God! I am so exhausted," said Olivia, wiping her face.

Cooper started taking long steps and asked Olivia to do the same. "It's nearby, let's be quick."

Olivia also followed Cooper, trying to keep her shoes safe from the dust all over. Soon they reached below the lamp post. There were street lights placed at equal distances and they were not sure if they worked or not. "Does it have current?" questioned Olivia.

"Look, it's glowing, but because of the sunlight, it's not visibly clear."

"So, where are we travelling?"

"We will go to the airport as planned, Rhythm would be waiting for us there," replied Cooper. He then took hold of Olivia's hand and they decided to say Avalonia together. They took a deep breath and said Avalonia, but before they could have completed the word, the bulb of the lamp post burst as if someone shot it from a distance. They both looked puzzled and looked to another lamp post in an array whose bulbs too started breaking with a shot.

"So we have a problem, Olivia," Cooper said, chagrined. Olivia looked at Cooper, who was looking to the other side, and saw Markboo walking between twenty Dslots, all wearing the black attire and black goggles. Their image was hazy due to the heat reflected on Earth, but it was clear that Markboo was too happy.

"Now it's crazy," said Olivia, bug-eyed.

Within no time, Markboo reached them with Dslots surrounding them. "Game over, Vslots. Go back to your school," Markboo said sarcastically.

"And what if we reject your suggestion?" said Cooper, giving a fierce look.

Markboo was all prepared and so he looked at the Dslot warrior standing along with him. The warrior immediately took a combat position. Before Cooper could take action, he heard a loud sound of someone falling. He turned to check and found Olivia sitting on the ground, with hair all over her face. She was too tired to fight again.

"Take me where you want, I am not moving an inch on my own," Olivia said.

Markboo just laughed and Cooper had all the reasons to surrender in front of him. He could not fight alone. Within no time, a truck reached the spot with an empty container. Dslots placed Cooper and Olivia inside and locked them in.

"In this place, you will not find a ray of hope. Let the documents reach Bernhard, I will leave you then," said Markboo, closing the door of the container. It was dark inside the box with no hope of light to enter. They placed the container at the extreme corner of the desert so that it could not be reached by any passer-by.

"Why should we not kill them?" questioned one of the Dslot warrior to Markboo.

Markboo smiled and then replied thoughtfully, "We are not interested in beginning a war. We only need Bernhard to complete his research."

Markboo started moving along with his warriors when he heard some sound. "Did you hear something?" Markboo questioned one of his warriors.

"I think they are struggling to come out," the warrior replied. Markboo smiled his winning smile and walked as he knew it was not an easy task to break it.

"Where are our guards, Cooper?" said a tired Olivia.

"Shut your mouth, Olivia. If you had not given up, we would not be stuck in here," Cooper said, trying to peep through the tough iron walls of the container. He paused and then turned, "They only come to help if we are dying. But here you are only enjoying as you are resting."

"So should I die?" said Olivia, making an innocent face.

"We need to think about it, Olivia. We are losing

time."

Suddenly something started striking the container, making a loud noise. "What the hell are they doing?" said Cooper.

"They are about to kill us, Cooper," said Olivia, afraid.

Milla Meets Rhythm

Rhythm took a path using a bulb to reach the airport. He waited outside and checked on the display board to confirm the arrival of her flight. He decided to meet her casually as if he was not aware of her visit. He moved to the local vendor and picked up a beer bottle and waited at the arrival section. His eyes were always at the arrival gate.

After some time, he saw Milla walking confidently towards the exit gate, holding a black bag in her hand. She looked gorgeous in her business attire. Rhythm saw her after days and wanted to run to her. But he had plans to not make her aware of his intentions. He placed the bottle back at the counter and started following her. Milla walked straight towards the parking lot to take a taxi. She raised her hand to stop one. As the cab was about to stop, Rhythm took quick steps to reach her and placed his hand on the door.

"I have booked this taxi," Milla said instantly, without noticing it's Rhythm.

"Oh my God! What are you doing here, Milla?" said Rhythm, acting as if he was not aware of her visit. She turned in astonishment and smiled, saying, "I must ask this. Where were you for the last two days? Boss was looking for you." She softly hugged him to greet him.

Rhythm made a serious face and then replied, "Uncle Gourd lost his aunty in Berlin, I was with him."

"Oh, I am sorry," she said with a sad face. "Why not talk in the cab? I am going to Williams Hotel near Aachen University," Milla said.

"What a surprise, Milla. I am also staying at the same hotel," Rhythm said. They both got into the taxi and then Rhythm questioned, "So why are you in Aachen?"

"Ah, actually, boss wanted to have some information about the extension plan for mobile technology which we recently tested. So he asked me to meet a few professors at Aachen University and take their viewpoints." Rhythm knew that she was not telling the truth and was sad about that as he always thought that she was his best friend.

She also asked a similar question to Rhythm, and he replied that he just came to visit the city as he was nearby. She smiled and then said, "I thought you were following me."

"You know something extraordinary happened in the flight," Milla said to Rhythm. Although Rhythm knew something happened because of Cooper and Olivia, he still questioned.

"There were thieves in the flight and they tried to take away my bag but thanks to some good people on board, they fought for me and somehow the door of the flight got opened and they flew away," Milla explained.

"It's serious, did they survive?" Rhythm questioned.

"I am not sure but my bag is safe. Airport authorities would be checking into the incident."

They reached the hotel in the next few minutes as it was nearby. As they got out of the cab, Rhythm tried to pick her bag but she immediately took it from his hand, saying, "I will manage Rhythm, no worries." Rhythm did not want to make her realize about his intentions and so he handed it over to her, smiling. They entered the hotel and moved to their respective rooms. Milla already had a room booked whereas Rhythm booked a room at that time. He confirmed to her that Uncle Gourd informed him about this hotel. On the stairs, Rhythm questioned her, "When are you meeting the professors?"

And she confirmed to him that the meeting was planned for the next day. As she reached the floor of her room, she said, "I would be going to the swimming pool after eight, you may join me. We can have dinner after that." Rhythm smiled at her and left as his room was one floor above hers.

Rhythm had a plan developing in his mind. He decided to enter her room when she would be at the pool and exchange the documents. That way, she would not know anything and he would be able to complete his task. He entered his room and lay down on the bed thinking about Cooper and Olivia. He was not aware of them and looked worried. He was eager to know their location and where they were stuck. He got up from the bed and reached the window to look outside. The view outside his window was fabulous. He was loving the atmosphere but looked tensed as time was running out and the sun was about to set.

On the other hand, Cooper and Olivia were struggling to get out of the container; they were locked. Markboo was very smart. He knew he cannot kill them so he locked them in a place from where they could not travel using a bulb. It had grown dark by then and they both could not even see themselves. "Cooper, I can feel Milla has reached," Olivia said as per intuitions that she was getting while Cooper was trying his best to look for a way out of that container. "What are you searching for, Cooper? We are stuck," said Olivia, depressed.

Cooper was thinking and then something clicked his mind. "I have a clock of Venus with me. I can travel in time to do something," replied Cooper, excitedly.

"But what will you do?"

Cooper, after scratching his head, asked her to wait. He set a time in his Venus clock and pressed the crown. Before Olivia could have questioned further, Cooper was back in time when Markboo was about to leave locking them inside the container.

"In this place, you will not find a ray of hope. Let the documents reach Bernhard, I will leave you then," said Markboo, closing the door of the container. It was dark inside the box with no hope of light to enter. Cooper, after travelling in time, hid safely behind the container and could listen to Markboo speaking.

As Markboo turned to move along with the warriors, Cooper looked around and then picked up a hard stone to strike the container and make a hole. Markboo heard the sound and turned back, asking his warrior, "Did you hear something?"

The warrior looked back and then replied, "I think they are struggling to come out." Markboo smiled his winning smile and walked as he knew it was not an easy task to break it.

"Where are our guards, Cooper?" said a tired Olivia.

"Shut your mouth, Olivia. If you had not given up, we would not be stuck in here," Cooper said, trying to peep through the tough iron walls of the container. He paused and then turned, "They only come to help if we are dying. But here you are only enjoying as you are resting."

"So should I die?" said Olivia, making an innocent face.

"We need to think about it, Olivia. We are losing time."

While Cooper and Olivia were discussing inside the container about the solution, Cooper, who travelled in time, was busy finding a solution to create a hole in the container, checking for weak points. After checking, he found a place at the top corner where a nut was placed. He decided to open that nut which could help them get a ray of hope. He moved down and threw that stone on top of the container, making a loud noise. Hearing that sound, Cooper inside the container said, "What the hell are they doing?"

Outside, he started striking the nut again and again to create a hole.

"They are about to kill us, Cooper," said Olivia, afraid, not knowing that it was Cooper who travelled in time and was creating the way out. Once Cooper was sure that the nut was loose enough, he used his fingers to unscrew it and then smiled after removing it. He then tried to peek inside through the hole and saw Olivia and himself struggling to get out. Cooper then jumped back and pressed the crown of the clock to go back in time.

Olivia observed the pixels combining back and looked happy as she knew that Cooper would have definitely made a way out. In the darkness of the container, she could only feel the pixels joining back and then she heard, "Olivia, I created a hole at the top left corner. We need to wait to get some help."

"But will you be able to go up there?" Olivia questioned. Cooper then explained to her that he saw an adjacent road, and they need to wait for any vehicle to pass by. As it was dark, they would be using a headlight and they can easily travel on seeing the ray of light through its bulb. The plan looked perfect to Olivia but she had a different question, "Why did you create a hole when you could have just opened the gate when you travelled in time?"

Cooper gave her a humiliating look and then said, "Olivia, I thought you knew Electon's rules perfectly, but let me explain it to you again." She was silent, and then he said, "When we travel in time, we cannot change the action which has been taken against us. We can only manipulate the sequence. As per Newton's law, every action has an equal and opposite reaction, and if we change the action in time which is already opposite in nature, the reaction could harm us."

Olivia now remembered and then said, "Sorry, I now remember it. Steven once explained this."

Cooper ignored her and started looking up at the hole that he had created. It was still dark outside. He tried placing his foot on the side, trying to climb out, but after a few attempts, he failed.

"I can try climbing your shoulders if you allow it," said Olivia, with a grave look on her face. Cooper looked thoughtful and then sat on his knees without saying a word, but Olivia understood she was to climb him. She then sat on his shoulders, crossing her legs on both sides of his neck. After realizing that she was comfortable, Cooper stood up, taking support on the sidewall. "Can you see anything?" Cooper questioned as Olivia placed her eye on the hole.

"Not yet, it's dark outside."

Cooper looked haunted as he was not sure until when he had to carry her on his shoulders. After a few minutes, she shouted, "I can see some light behind the plateau. It's approaching us."

"Fantastic, keep monitoring and once you see it clearly, say Avalonia. We will say it together to reach Aachen," Cooper replied, excited and anxious. Olivia glued her eyes on the hole monitoring the movement of the far approaching light. "It's approaching, Cooper."

After a few minutes, she saw a white truck taking a roundabout from behind the plateau. She could hear the sound of the song playing in the loneliness of the highway. And then she said, "Cooper, the truck will take a right and its headlight will be straight towards the container. That would be a perfect time. Say Avalonia on the count of three."

Cooper was all ready and set to travel. He was worried and didn't want to miss the chance and then she started the countdown. Cooper was all set and then when she said three, they chanted the magical word together.

Time To Take Away

Roger picked up the phone in his room and dialled the number of Milla's room. He wanted to ensure that she had left for the swimming pool. After a few rings were unanswered, he walked to the window to wait for some more time. He was sad that her best friend lied to him, but he was more concerned about his task and his new friends, Cooper and Olivia. After waiting for a few more minutes, he dialled the same number again. He wanted to ensure that she was not in her room. Once the call got disconnected, he was sure that she had left. He put on his T-shirt, which he had removed to relax in his room and then opened his door carefully, ensuring that he was not being followed by any Dslots. He closed his door and took the stairs to reach the floor below. He carefully monitored his movements and arrived safely outside her room. To double-check, he first knocked at the door, but when Milla didn't answer, he took a step back to let the door open after chanting Avalonia. The door latch turned on its own and the door opened a little. "Bonzer," he said, smiling and walked inside quietly.

Rhythm started looking around for the black bag that she was carrying along with her. He removed the blanket, turned the suitcase, and opened the door of the cupboard. But he could not find the bag. He looked around confused and then leaned to check below the bed. There he saw a bag safely placed at a corner. He knew why she put it at such a place. He moved his hand by stretching it and then smiled as he took hold of its strip. "I got you," he said. He pulled the bag and kissed it, bringing it closer to his face and then pulled himself up supporting himself on his knees.

"You should have asked me directly, Rhythm," said Milla, leaning on the wall, wearing a white swimming parka.

Rhythm was shocked hearing her voice. Inscrutable, he looked above and then said, "Nothing like that Milla. I was just trying to surprise you and then realized that your bag was lying under the bed so tried to keep it safe." She continued looking at him with glowering eyes and snatched the bag after taking a step towards him.

She then turned and walked to another side. Rhythm was trying to explain to her, "Listen Milla, you are taking me wrong." But before he could conclude his explanation, she turned. She put her right palm in front of her and her left to the back and said, "Slay." A blue firelight fired from her hand and hit Rhythm on his chest, throwing him to the other side of the room and causing him to hit the wall. Rhythm was not expecting something like that from Milla. It was a shock to him as he tried to gather strength in him while pressing his chest to stand. Milla confidently walked towards him, taking slow steps, and then removed the parka to flaunt her figured body with a blue outfit of a Dslot. "You did as we wanted, Rhythm," said Milla sarcastically, and then continued, "Dslots are very powerful and we knew what next would be in the list of tasks for Vslots." She paused and continued, "We were well-prepared from days."

She came near Rhythm and placed her fingers over his face, saying, "Markboo intentionally took you to the Electon world as we knew it was only you who could drill down to such a level of detail and would help us to know the origin of frequency duplexing; you presented me your skills in the telecom company during the first mobile call."

Rhythm now gathered strength and stood up taking the support of the wall. "But how were you so sure that I would be involved in this task?" Rhythm questioned Milla with wet eyes as he felt betrayed.

Milla smiled, "Steven, our Dslot. He convinced Noah by showing him our friendship in the molten glass blow and suggested that you would be best to take away the logic from me."

"I always knew it was Steven," Rhythm said in pain.

Milla now took a step towards him and then continued, "I hope I could kill you but it's not possible for us. That's the reason we decided to keep you captive and we were successful."

Rhythm was still confused and questioned, "But why did you want to keep me captive? What will you get out of that?"

"You don't know anything about this world, Rhythm. You don't know how important you are for Vslots and the devil Noise. Any negotiation can happen to you," Milla answered with a jeering look. She again walked to him and said, "You still need to learn a lot, Rhythm."

Milla gave a flirty look and continued, "Markboo was never a fool. He intentionally brought you to this world and let you reach Arch Rotunda. We already had Steven in Arch, who successfully passed on all the information about your findings, which you and your team did to analyze about Samuel Morse."

"But Steven welcomed Bumblebee in the Arch who was supposed to kill me?"

"I am not sure about why Steven did that; as you know, you can never trust anyone in Electon. But our purpose was solved, that is what we needed."

Rhythm was downcast and felt lost. She looked at him confidently and raised her hand to take him captive. "He may be new to the world but we Vslots are here to protect him," said Cooper, who appeared from the light bulb hanging on the ceiling above the centre table behind Milla, and without warning, he fired a purple firelight from his hands, hitting Milla from behind. It hit her. She was hurt and broke the mirror placed on the cupboard as she fell on it. Rhythm immediately felt confident and jumped towards Cooper while Milla turned to fire at him from the ground. But this time, Olivia was ready to take up the challenge. The firelight of Milla and Olivia collided to create a massive light. There was a loud sound and a lot of heat in the room. Rhythm turned his face to avoid the flare while Cooper covered Rhythm and fired towards Milla, hitting her again, making her roll to a side.

Rhythm then picked up the bag and rushed towards the window. He threw a flower vase at the glass window to break it and then looked down. He was surprised that it was too high for him to jump. Milla and Olivia were still busy shooting flares at each other, and then suddenly, pixels started to appear in the room. "Rhythm, it's time to run," said Cooper, looking at those pixels. Without alerting Rhythm, Cooper held him by his neck and jumped from the window. Olivia turned to check on them, fired a final shot and jumped after them.

"Go and get them," shouted Milla to the other Dslots who had just appeared in the room. Hearing her, those Dslots too jumped from the window, followed by Milla. Rhythm was running in front, holding the bag in his hand. His breath came in small spurts, hot and nervous. Cooper was running behind him, jumping over all the things that came in his path, and then he turned to fire a purple shot, which was known as immolate in Electon. Olivia was doing the same but Dslots behind her were quick enough to save themselves from their attacks. Milla jumped over the waste bags that crossed her path and fired her blue fireball at Olivia. Olivia tried to dodge the shot, but undoubtedly, the next fireball hit her on her chest, making her fly to a distance and struck her on a pillar. The five Dslots, along with Milla, were swiftly trying to catch up to them. Cooper was now not only concerned about the task but also to save Rhythm, who was not aware of the powers he carried. Cooper and Olivia were trying their best to cover Rhythm, who was running without a break, taking swift turns.

One of the Dslots jumped over the car parked to the side of the wet road and flew towards Cooper. But Cooper was swift to punch him hard, twisting him in the air and making him fall down hard. Cooper now stopped where he was, ready to take the Dslots one on one. Another Dslot arrived at his side and punched him on his face, but Cooper turned back and slammed his face.

Another Dslot threw his body weight behind the fist that edged closer to Olivia's face. It hit her jaw with such a force that blood pooled into her mouth. Pain erupted at the point of impact. With both her hands, Olivia then grasped his head in her hands and struck his nose with her knee. There was a blunt crack and then she released his dark-haired head. Blood oozed from both his nostrils and his nose was twisted right. He drew his fist back and punched her stomach; it was like hitting a train head-on. Olivia's guts smashed together, but she repaid him for it by punching his jaw. She continued this battering until he fell to the floor. His chest gently rose and sank with each shallow breath he drew in. Olivia observed him dropping with a glowering look and then turned to bring another one down.

But this time, it was Milla who fired her immolate towards her, and Olivia got hit. On the other hand, Rhythm reached a dead end and had no other place to run. He looked at all sides to find a way out. Olivia fell on the ground and fell unconscious as her head hit the ground. Cooper was alone, struggling, firing, and punching Dslots. Milla then walked confidently towards Cooper while he was engrossed in the fight and then from the closer distance, she said, "Sclerous," placing her hand over his head. That was the word that would harden the tissues of the body, and so Cooper lost all his force and started struggling even to raise his hand. He tried to punch Milla but his hand was not able to even reach her face. Milla smiled, saying, "You need to study hard, Vslots." She then punched Cooper, causing him to fall on the floor.

Rhythm was confused. He was holding the bag in his hand and was not sure what to do next. He was surrounded by other Dslots and Milla. "Throw that bag to me, Rhythm," said Milla, peeved. Rhythm tightened his fist to hold the bag tight. "You must obey, my dear," she said, smiling. Rhythm knew it was a lost game and he needs to surrender. After staring at her for a few seconds, he threw the bag towards her but while the bag was in the air, Rhythm heard a word, "Ensnare," and the bag caught fire. He looked behind Milla and saw Eva in the air with her right leg in front and chanting the word. A sudden smile emerged on Rhythm's face. Milla turned and was astonished to see Eva. Milla had not expected her to be there.

Before Milla could have understood, Eva chanted 'Regelate', throwing a white light towards Cooper. This word was used as an antidote to 'Sclerous'. Cooper was not ready to lose the chance, and he immediately stood up and punched the Dslot standing next to him. Eva then touched the ground and said, "Squander," while punching Milla. That spell threw Milla in the air to about fifty-meters and banged her head on the lamp post.

"I have studied very hard, Dslots," said Eva, all set to fight them. Eva was known as one of the most studious among all the Vslots and her knowledge about magical words was fabulous. Rhythm immediately ran to her and hugged her, saying, "I knew you were correct."

Milla pressed her head and then tried to get up in pain, but she was not ready to give up. Milla closed her eyes and spread both her hands, trying to gather energy from the electromagnetic waves around. A blue sphere of light gathered near her palm as she opened her eyes. But before she could have thrown it at Eva, they all heard a loud noise from another side as if some massive body was coming running towards them causing everything in its path to crush. They all turned their face in that direction to check what the sound was all about and was terrified to see Bumblebee coming running towards them furiously. Finding him rushing towards them, Rhythm took hold of Eva's hand and jumped towards Olivia. Cooper also rushed and took hold of their hands, and then Rhythm shouted, "Escutcheon Charon." As he chanted the word, a shield got developed around them with the dust of Pluto. Finding them protected, Bumblebee now turned towards Milla and rushed towards her. He picked her up in his hands and the last thing Rhythm could hear was Milla shouting in pain.

'Escutcheon Charon' created a shield with the dust of Pluto, which Pluto got from its moon, Charon. "You knew this?" asked Eva, still holding Rhythm's hand.

"This is the only spell I read from the Electon spellbook," Rhythm smiled to reply.

Cooper hugged Eva and so did Olivia, welcoming her back, and they thanked her for saving them. "We must go back to Arch as our task is over. Documents were burnt along with the bag," said Cooper. They all smiled and took hold of their hands to look at the bulb of the lamp post to say Avalonia. Within no time, their body started evaporating into pixels, circled, and entered the lamp post. Although they were happy about completing the task, Rhythm was upset thinking about Milla. She had been his friend for years and he had been only apprehensive about her grandmother.

On their way back, Rhythm looked confused as he had not read Escutcheon Charon from the Electon Spellbook, but this spell was told to him by Greg.

After meeting Emma to understand about crushed Pisanki, Greg pulled Roger behind the pillar when he was on his way to meet Cooper.

"Is all fine, sir?" Roger questioned.

Greg gave him an agonized look and then said, "Escutcheon Charon, remember this word."

Roger was quizzical and questioned after a pause, "But what is this?"

Greg gave a strict look to say, "The Son of the Queen asks too many questions. Learn to follow what is said and try not to present yourself as the King of Electon." He gave a grave look to Roger and then started walking, but stopped at some distance, turned and said, "You may need this to save someone from the devil Noise."

Roger was confused and was not able to understand

the reason why he had been asked to learn that spell but he remembered and tried to use it when he found Bumblebee attacking them. He realized on his way back that he needs to understand Greg a little more.

How Did Eva Return?

Noah looked quizzical after not finding the molten glass bowl in the cabin of Steven. It was a matter of concern for him. He knew conspiracies are a part of Electon and it had happened many times to change the future. He closed his eyes, spreading his hands, which he usually did to contact someone who helped and guided him whenever he needed a suggestion. He then opened his eyes and said, "I need to move in time to get answers and bring egalitarianism for Eva if she is correct." Emma nodded and said that in the meantime, she would try to contact Quodtophet and ask them to stop interrogating Eva as it was very painful.

Emma opened the door and walked fast in the corridor, flapping her gown. She ran to the end of the corridor and jumped from the edge, flipping her dress to her face and in a blink of an eye, she vanished in the air.

Noah closed his eyes again and then pressed the crown of his Venus clock. Within no time, he found himself in the athenaeum. He looked around and saw Eva conversing with Sita. He walked closer to listen to what they were up to. Eva looked concern. "If Samuel has created a frequency duplexing document, it must be available in athenaeum. How come it's missing?"

"I am totally not aware. It must be available. Need to look into the matter," said Sita, peeved as she could not understand how it happened.

Noah immediately understood what could be the reason as per his experience. He set a new time in his Venus clock and pressed the crown, to reach the time when Samuel Morse received the document from Charles Wheatstone... He found Samuel reading that document under the candlelight totally glued to it. Noah walked to have a look at the paper and reached behind him. Then, adjusting his spectacles, he leaned to have a look at the document. He was correct that the document was written with blue ink by Charles, which stated how electrical signals can be used to transmit messages using different frequencies for sending and receiving.

Noah was busy reading when Samuel said, without looking at Noah, "Noah, you can come into the light and read it along with me."

It was a shock to Noah as he was not aware that Samuel could see him. Samuel then placed his hand in his pocket to get the dust out and spread it over Noah. Noah closed his eyes and realized that he was visible to him.

"You can see me, Samuel?" said Noah, confused.

Samuel now stood up and turned towards him, saying, "Yes, I can."

Noah gave a strange look seeing which Samuel explained, "I am not a technical guy but still developing technology, you know how?" He took a pause and started folding the document, and then continued, "On my way back to my home town, I met someone who travelled to Earth from a distant planet. They are the ones who monitor each and every movement over our world and teach us to explore more. It's because of them we are learning new things each day and developing our community on this planet." Samuel smiled and took a pause to continue, "It's because of them, I could decide on developing a telegraph, and it's because of them, I came to know about Electon."

"This is a surprise for me, Samuel," said Noah.

"You would be surprised to know that in the human world, you can explore Saturn rings because you once lived on Saturn many many years ago and this information was also given to me by them. They told me that one day you will come to know about this document." Samuel took a step towards Noah and then said, looking deep into his eyes in his adenoidal voice, "This document will lead to the reign of Dslots and the end of the human race in the future. If I keep it with me, a copy will be created in the athenaeum, which is never safe in there. Better you take it with you and hide it in the most reliable place where no one can reach it ever."

Samuel explained to him that if the document is directly moved to Electon, there will be no copy of it in the human world so no reproduction in athenaeum. It's a way to play with the process to keep Electon safe from Dslots.

"But how could you see me as I travelled in time and humans cannot see time travellers?" Noah questioned.

Samuel rolled the document and then explained, "This power was given to me by the person whom I met from the distant planet. He sprinkled water over my face stating that the water was from Europa, one of the moons of Jupiter. Europa receives the maximum amount of electromagnetic waves due to reflection from Jupiter and so it's water has a property that can help me see people from Electon. Dslots are clever; they travelled in time when Europa had sources of that water and developed their own modified version of Venus clocks."

Dslot's in the future of Electon have an advanced clock of Venus, which has a mix of water from Europa in it. That's the reason why when Dslots travel in time, they can be seen by others but it is totally dependent on them if they want to be visible or not.

Noah understood what he was explaining, and then said, "Didn't those people tell you about the future? Will Dslots come?"

Samuel smiled and then picked up a paper on which Morse code was written. "It all depends on how you manage Arch Rotunda. My purpose is to support Anagol by developing a telegraph and give Electon a new avenue called the telegraph. The rest of it is on the coming generations."

Noah understood his words and knew what he had to do. Noah took those documents, thanked him, and moved back to the same time when Eva was moving out from the athenaeum to meet Steven.

She crossed the corridor, holding a book about the telegraph in her hand. She looked calm and steady as she walked. Her facial expression had no evidence of a big plan. She reached outside the cabin of Steven and knocked at the door. "Hello, my dear Eva, pleasant to see you," Steven said as he opened the door.

"Sir, I have a few questions, I hope you won't mind helping me with them?" Eva said politely. Steven happily welcomed her inside his cabin. Noah also moved inside, not knowing that at the same time, Roger was also in the room as he had travelled in time. Steven offered her a cup of tea and then asked her about her doubt.

"Sir, I am on a task," Eva started, but Steven added before she concluded, "Along with Cooper and the son of the Queen."

"Exactly!" she replied and added, "I read journals in athenaeum and came to know that Samuel Morse got help from Charles Wheatstone for his invention about the telegraph. But Charles was busy inventing Wheatstone bridge at the time when he supported him. I feel that the Wheatstone bridge has something to do in this task."

Noah followed them silently and wanted to check what Steven had done. He carefully listened to the conversation which was about the Wheatstone bridge. As Steven offered her the tea of truth, Noah took a step calmly and smelled the tea and immediately understood that it had a crushed limestone that was found on the planet, Mars, used by Mayas to take control over brain cells.

Wise men from Maya civilization were in contact with the leftover people of Mars. They were in the last days of the Electon of Mars in those times. Many humans from Mars were regularly travelling to Earth for safe shelter because after Dslots took over Mars, the planet was on the verge of extinction. The people of Mars carried limestone from Mars, which they used on the humans of Earth to control their brain cells and used to make them think that they are God and tried to motivate Maya civilization people to do as they wished. Being highly civilized and technology-equipped, they also helped the humans of Earth to grow and develop. Later, Maya civilization people also used these limestones for the same purpose to rule Earth. Steven was using the same limestone.

Steven then shifted the Pisanki in his room to enter the room where Venus clocks were placed. He picked up Eva in his arms and put her in the room between the clocks.

"Sorry, Eva, but someone needs to be sacrificed for the change," Steven said while picking up the Venus clock. It was clear to Noah that it was Steven who took control over her brain cells and made her do the changes in the arithmetic logic of the Hertzonia gate. But he was still not sure about the story which Steven narrated to him about Eva applying encrypted codes over him to make him sleep. Noah took a step back, and unfortunately, his hand slipped the photo frame placed on the side table there. He wanted to verify the story which Steven narrated to him about Eva, and so he walked along with Steven.

Eva was sleeping when Steven picked up the Venus clock and then, standing in front of her, he closed his eyes to say, "Cerebrum." Cerebrum was the chant used to hypnotize a person and make him or her do what one wants.

"You are a soldier of Dslot whose aim is to erase the son of the Queen from this world. Reach Hertzonia to help Bumblebee enter this Arch," said Steven as Eva opened her eyes unblinkingly.

Noah now understood that whatever story Steven narrated to him about Eva was false and he only did it to keep himself safe and let Eva face the consequences if the plan failed.

Noah stepped out of the room and decided to first place the documents in a safe place before helping Eva. He stepped out of the room and closed his eyes, spreading both his hands to listen to his inner voice. But one mistake Noah did was that he left Steven there without monitoring what he did next.

Noah then remembered that in Arch Rotunda, at the far most corner behind the forest of wires was an old telegraph room, which had been created because the telegraph had been invented in the human world by Samuel. As no one visits that place, it was safest to hide it there. He took long steps to reach behind the Arch and then started walking across the wired forest, which was the darkest forest of Electon. That forest had huge trees which had wires as its branches. Because of that dense web of cables, it was called 'the copper forest'. Noah gripped the document and walked safely, avoiding the juggling up in the wires which could cause him to die if he got trapped in there. His eyebrows shrank in tension and his golden hair moved in the breeze as he walked all alone safely. He safely moved the web of cables in front of him to see the telegraph room, which stood all alone between the jungle. It was an old, rusted, iron box-shaped small room with a rusted iron door closed with a circular ring. Being in Arch for ages, all wires entangled all over the place. It looked as if they had taken over the room. Noah walked, finding the best place to place his foot, and finally reached the entrance gate of the telegraph room.

He stood and checked to see a way out to open the door without disturbing the cables. He then placed the folded documents in his overcoat pocket and took hold of the circular ring to open the door. The ring was stuck having been closed for ages. Noah applied his strength to twist it anticlockwise to open it, and then with a shrilling sound, it opened. Since it had been closed for decades, cables had taken over its inside too. Noah looked all around and then pulled a cigar from his pocket and said, "Relume." Relume was a chant that was used in Electon to get a firelight. Noah always carried a cigar which was his light in the dark. As he chanted the word, a fire lit on the upper part of the cigar, which was enough for him to have a look at the safest place inside. He then walked safely to avoid any mishap. After walking for some distance inside, he saw an iron door cupboard. He opened the same. It was dirty and webbed but looked safe to place the documents in as no one would ever think of coming in there. Noah then took the documents back from his overcoat and put them safely inside. He closed the door and moved back, taking the same path by which he came to the telegraph room. His return was quick as he knew which way had to be taken; he had to reach Hertzonia to save Roger.

"Noah, we need you urgently," said Steven, reaching Noah in time, when he just entered his cabin. Noah knew what he was up to, but still, he questioned to verify.

"Eva played a game with me. She is inspired by Dslots, I doubted her since she did her last task. She was too attracted by Oryut. She took away the clock of Venus by applying the encrypted code over me."

Noah listened carefully although he knew what he was going to narrate and then said, "Hand over the Venus clock to me, I'll see what is to be done. Meanwhile, you must go to Greg. He must need you."

Steven did as he was told. He handed over the clock and moved to Greg, not knowing that Greg was all ready for him. Noah then pressed the crown of the clock to reach Hertzonia to save Roger.

Noah knew clearly what he was supposed to do. He rushed to Hertzonia and saved Roger and ordered the red warriors to take Eva to Quodtophet. Although he knew that Eva was not a culprit, he ordered it to ensure the safety of Electon. Also, he did not want Steven to know that he now knew his plans. He was interested in catching Steven red-handed and knowing what he was planning further.

Noah then pressed the crown of the Venus clock

to come back to the real-time. He immediately walked up to Greg, whom he had already informed to call red warriors to arrest Steven but Noah was surprised as Steven never reached him. "Where is Steven, Greg?" Noah questioned with folded hands.

"Sorry, my lord. I took your orders and the red warriors are waiting in hiding, but Steven never turned up," Greg replied languidly.

Noah was now able to understand the multiple changes which he had seen in the Arch since days and followed the intensions of Steven, as no one in the Arch could unfollow his words. "I have something urgent to check. You ask the warriors to search for Steven at any cost," ordered Noah to Greg.

"As you say, Noah."

The red warriors then came out from their hideout and took a sinusoidal curve in the air to reach every corner of Arch Rotunda in search of Steven. While Noah took long steps to go back to the telegraph room, he doubted if those documents had been stolen by Steven. He opened the iron cupboard and saw that the documents had been taken away. "Why, Steven, why? Your actions will take Earth to a new hell," said Noah in pain.

When Noah ordered Steven to meet Greg, he actually went to his own cabin first and smiled thinking of the mistake Noah did by not capturing him at the right time. "I am such a good actor; the ancient Noah got fooled," Steven said, smiling, looking at the molten glass bowl. He wanted to know what Noah was up to as he understood that Noah had travelled in time. He crushed one Pisanki long back, which is a method to transport an error in the time travel scenarios. Pisanki was made up of multiple colours which resembled pixels. Crushing Pisanki meant destroying a few of those pixels. Those crushed pixels then keep trying to move along with the person, but the person gets stuck at the same time travel room. Being in charge of the time travel room, Steven could easily monitor those paths. He safely watched the way of Roger, Cooper, Eva, Olivia, and also Noah and knew that Noah was travelling to various time zones in search of the documents. And when he realized that Noah came back from the time of Samuel, the picture was clear to him.

"Tell me, my molten glass bowl, what the idiot Noah is up to now," said Steven, writing the details of Noah on a paper when Noah was on his way to the forest of wires. He looked curiously as Noah took the dangerous path to the telegraph room and finally was able to get the location of the frequency duplexing documents. Once he was assured that Noah had placed the documents in the iron cupboard, he took the same path to the forest of wires and took the molten glass bowl along with him so that he could keep an eye on Noah's actions.

Steven safely walked outside the Arch, keeping an eye to be safe from each administrative personnel. He held the bowl in both his hands while walking between the web of wires. His face was glowing blue because of the reflection from the water of the bowl as he reached the telegraph room. He then safely placed the bowl down at the corner of the room and started trying to clear the road, not knowing that the wires had begun to move slowly to grab the bowl. The wires began elongating from all sides to create a web to take away the molten glass bowl. Steven then entered the room as the door opened and turned to pick the bowl back but was shocked to see that the wires had become active and were taking up the bowl in the air. Each of the wire was trying to take that bowl in its own control making the water pour all over the place. "Oh, shit," Steven said, making a peeved face. He adjusted his dress and then turned to walk inside the room. That bowl was helpful for him but he was more interested in getting the documents for which he had planned everything. He placed his feet carefully as it was dark and he could not see anything, but he knew the direction and the location of the document.

"My dear wires, please be quiet and do not harm me," he said in a brittle voice as he walked. With his hands, he tried to touch the walls on his side to get the cupboard handle in his hand. "I wish I had a cigar of light with me."

After walking for a few more steps, he reached the cupboard. "Here you are, my dear. Googol would be too happy with me," said Steven pleasantly, as he opened the door and picked the documents.

He laughed out loud, hugging the documents as he brought them near his chest, and then moved his right hand back in the pocket of his overcoat to bring out the clock of Venus. He planned to move to the future of Electon and handover those documents to Googol. "How to set the time in this darkness? Let me make the approximation," said Steven, rolling the dice of the Venus clock and then pressed the crown, saying, "Hope I land in the correct time." Electon had never seen the light of Sun, and the copper forest was darker and denser.

Emma, on the other hand, reached Quodtophet on time. The bottle in which Eva was placed was about to be burned in the furnace of hell. "Eva needs to be released, she is innocent," said Emma, tensed, to Venroot. Venroot was the head of Quodtophet and documented each and every detail of each Vslot in Electon. He was the one who was supposed to get the interrogations to take place and all red warriors reported to him.

He was a man with a unique personality. His head was more significant than his body, so he was assumed to be very intelligent. He used to write with all his six hands at the same time, and he always found it challenging to sit because of his long hairy tail. He looked perfect in his black attire which had a hole in his pants to allow the tail to reach out.

"You people will definitely make me a culprit someday by making me punish someone innocent," he said in his gravelly voice.

"I am sorry, Venroot, but the investigation has taken another turn," Emma said and then continued with a pause, "hope you would help in recovery?"

He looked at her with a grave look, placing his chin over his entangled fingers, and then said to the red warrior standing to his side, "Get the lady out of the bottle and bring her here."

The red warrior nodded and walked inside the room behind him. The Quodtophet was not a pleasant place to visit. It was made up of dark red colour stones, with walls fabricated with iron ore for protection. The fire lamps placed at each corner elaborated its dirty beauty. The floor and wall had blood sprinkled all over it, giving it a look of hell. The wall behind the Venrootwas decorated with the heads of the Vslots who got punished in the past. Blood from a few of those heads could still be seen flowing. Emma looked up at one of the heads which looked fresh. "Oh! He was an agent of Vslots on the new planet which had similarities to Earth but started supporting Dslots as they wanted to be the first ones on that planet. We caught him and now look how handsome he looks on my wall," Venroot said, smiling.

Emma gave a scowling look as she hated blood. Soon

the red warrior walked back, holding the glass bottle in her hand in which Eva was captive and placed it on the table of Venroot. Emma looked with her pitying eyes as she could understand the pain Eva might be in. She took a step towards the bottle but Venroot stopped her. He then opened the bottle and blew soft air with his mouth over it. As his breath reached inside the bottle, the pixels inside started to glow with multiple colours revolving and then began to come out of the bottle forming Eva. Within a few seconds, Eva was visible in front of Emma as she lay on the floor devasted, lethargic, and tired. Emma rushed to her, going on her knees to place her hand on her forehead, caressing her to make her feel comfortable. "You are fine, my child," Emma said, trying to help her back to stand.

"I am innocent, Emma," Eva said in a very sotto voice.

"We know, Eva, be calm."

Eva tried to open her eyes slowly and then questioned, "Where are my teammates? They need me."

Emma held her shoulders and replied, "They are still on task, but you need to take care now."

"No, Emma. If I am not a part of the task, I would never come out of the pain of being an anti-Electon. Please help me know where my friends are."

Emma looked into her eyes and knew how vital that task was for her and so, she informed her about their location. Eva, after listening to the exact details, requested Emma to take her to the Alva room so that she could travel to the human world to protect her friends and help them in completing the task. Emma knew the feelings of a true Vslot and she could not let her down. Emma took her to the Alva room and helped her to travel to the human world.

Googol Pleasure

It was silent on the open pathway of Mount View, California, in the future of Electon. Only the sound of beetles could be heard in the vegetation spread all around. The pathway was illuminated by fire lamps placed at equal distances as it was dark. There was thunder and it seemed like it would rain. Green clouds were gathering over Mount View as they knew some historical change was about to happen in the world of Electon.

The pixels started to gather on the lonely street and within no time, Steven appeared with the documents hidden in his coat. He looked worried and afraid as he knew Vsot warriors could reach him anytime. Every single sound was terrifying him, which was evident on his haunted face. He was not sure where he landed in the darkness. His only motto at that moment was to meet Googol and handover the documents to him.

He started walking towards the north, terrified, looking in all directions as he took quick steps. Time to time, he stopped and looked around, ensuring he was still all alone, and then again walked fast. After walking for a little while, he managed to check the signboard, which was hidden behind the bushes. He immediately stepped down from the road, still haunted with the sound of thunder, and then walked between the tall grass. He carefully moved the bushes and tried to read what was written as it was dark. It showed a right turn for Googolplex. Steven smiled, finding that he was in the correct place. He reached back to the road and started to walk fast. He wanted to reach there as quickly as possible.

While he was walking, he heard the sound of someone's feet from a distance. He soon understood that someone was approaching him. He started walking much faster than before, wiping his sweat from his forehead. The footsteps began to echo louder as if they were about to reach him. Steven understood that it was time to hide, and so he jumped to the side of the road and crawled, crossing the long grass to reach the thorny bushes.

Intimidated, he watched the intruder and then saw three Dslot warriors riding over a neodymium Equine. Equine is a type of horse that is known to be very smart and energetic. In the future of Electon, these Equine were made up of neodymium, a component of misch metal and some other alloys. A digital display unit was visible on the neck of the Equine, which could recognize intruders by creating their thermal image over it. Dslot warriors kept an eye on that screen to know where the intruders were hiding. Their tail was ultrasonic sensitive and could detect any single movement around them which could be dangerous. Their body was connected with multiple circuitry boards and mechanical pulleys, which rotated and helped them gain inertia to move fast without friction.

The Dslot warriors were tall, with perfect physique, and wore their traditional blue metallic dress, with golden-brown hair which reached their shoulders. They were riding those neodymium Equines. As they reached closer to Steven, the warrior in the front raised his right hand, gesturing others to stop. He noticed some thermal images on his screen and wanted to check on the intruder.

Finding them near, Steven started pushing his body backward, trying to go out of sight of the Equine to avoid his thermal image. Steven wanted to meet Googol but was not sure if these warriors would take him to Googol or would arrest him and take him to the Quodtophet of the future. So he preferred to hide.

"Is anyone out there?" questioned one of the warriors. The warrior at the front was glued to the screen and then replied, "Saw some thermal image but then lost it."

"Maybe some animal?"

The warrior at the front then turned his Equine back to face the other warriors and said, "The thundering is not as usual." As he turned, the tail of Equine picked the ultrasonic sound of Steven and gave the indication of an intruder. The warrior immediately turned in action. "Someone is here for sure," he shouted and took hold of his Equine to move downward. Steven understood that his movement has been noticed and he needs to hasten to save himself. He stood and rushed backward among the bushes, but the warriors were quick and immediately surrounded him from all sides with Steven standing in between them – sweating and hiding the documents.

"You look like a Vslot? Capture him, warriors," shouted one of them.

"Bruvver, bruvver… I am your friend," Steven shouted, partially closing his eyes in fear.

"Prove it, prowler," the warrior showed his sword to him and shouted.

Steven, still with his hands up in a surrendering

position, said in his wheezy sound, "Take me to Googol, and if he punishes me, I'll go with you."

"Why to the lord?"

"Because I am his emissary," Steven replied.

The warriors looked at each other as they knew if they killed the emissary of Googol, he would be angry. "Should we?" one of the warriors questioned the others. Listening to him, the others nodded.

"Hand over your clock and anything suspicious in your pockets," the warrior said.

Snarling, Steven immediately took the stuff out and handed everything over to the warrior of the Equine. "What more are you hiding? Handover that too."

"It's for Lord Googol, no one is allowed to touch it. It's harmless, just a roll of paper," Steven confirmed, with fear over his face. He wanted to keep the documents safe with himself.

The warriors looked at each other and then said, "Start walking in front of us and let me remind you, we are just behind." Steven nodded innocently and started walking, taking small steps, still safely holding the documents. The lonely road echoed with the footsteps of the Equine and the breath of Steven, who was tired walking in front.

Steven smiled as he saw the full campus walls of the castle of Googol. The warriors stepped from the Equine and then tied them to the holders at the side of the main gate of the Googleplex. The size of the warriors was massive, about ten feet taller. The warriors then took him along with them to the central court where Googol was available.

"My lord, he says he is your emissary," the warrior said, going down on his knees while Googol stood in front, smiling.

"Time knows how to mature brains to bring an evolution in nature," Googol said in his crocky voice, took a few steps, and reached closer to Steven. "Well done, Steven, and welcome to the world of Dslots," Googol said, presenting his hand for the document.

Steven smiled and gave an arrogant look to the warriors and then brought the documents out from his coat and placed it in the hands of Googol.

"My, my, my... you made it so simple, Steven," Googol said pleased, holding the frequency duplexing documents in his hands.

"Time will come for you to get rewarded as a Dslot. Till then, your safety is important," Googol said and then turned to another side, "You must hide in the human world presently. Stay there calm and quiet, until time needs you back in Electon."

"My lord, as you suggest," said Steven, downcast.

Googol then looked at the documents, smiled, and said, "So as the documents moved to the Electon world by Noah, Milla's bag got empty." Googol looked thoughtful and then continued, "So none of the documents got burned in her bag." He smiled again, understanding the situation and then added, "Milla, your sacrifice was not wasted, my dear."

Steven was highly inspired by Oryut, a Dslot, when he met him during his task a few years back in Poland. He started believing that Dslots were the future of Electon. His thought process changed after that task. He started considering Dslots to be the way of development for mankind. When he visited Poland, he realized how important it is to reduce distances and build a strong network of communication so that information from various parts of Earth can be shared with everyone. But he never knew that Oryut was a warrior of Googol and he always planned his task in advance. Googol planted Oryut on the mission to inspire Vslots so that he can use them when needed and Steven actually paid off the same idea of Googol.

The Bernhard Castle

The Alva room was lost in its own silence in the dim lights of the fire lamps when the Alva bulb started to glow again, flickering and spreading light as pixels began coming out of it. Soon, the sound of laughter and happiness echoed in the room as Roger, Cooper, Eva, and Olivia appeared in the room. "Without Eva, it would not have been a success," said Roger, smiling and walking out of the room.

"Exactly. Your entry was a surprise for them," added Olivia.

They opened the door and saw Noah standing at the edge of the floor, gazing outside. They all went silent, finding him on the floor and then walked towards him with respect, to inform him about the success. Noah was looking outside, lost in his own thoughts, and didn't notice them coming.

"Sir, dedicated thoughts and effective action can make anything a success; you said it once," Cooper said from behind him, interrupting the silence of Noah. Noah turned in surprise.

"Oh! My children, you are back," Noah said and then looked in the eyes of Eva. He didn't look buoyant. Eva understood something was not perfect and so she questioned, "Are you not happy with the success, sir?"

Noah now turned back to look outside and then showed them something by raising his finger. All four of them took a step to gather around him to check what he was looking at. They were confounded after seeing the enormous blue chateau at a far distance from Arch Rotunda. From that floor, they could see a massive number of people walking in a queue to the main gate of the blue chateau to take entry. The chateau was enormous and was shining blue as it had been constructed newly in Electon.

"What is that, sir?" questioned Olivia, bug-eyed.

Noah paused and looked scowling and said, "The entry of Dslots in present Electon." He paused and then continued, "The castle of Bernhard."

"What? But we destroyed the documents," said Cooper in astonishment, and added, "how come they succeeded?"

Noah again turned towards them and then answered, "Some mistakes we do unintentionally which are planned in that way to be completed." Noah took a pause and placed his hand on Roger's shoulder to continue, "Remember, we can lose a battle but if we have hope, no battle is ever lost."

Roger nodded after looking deep into his eyes.

"They have entered our world, but we have hope to vanish them out," added Noah, with confidence and in a motivating tone.

"We will, Noah," said Eva, followed by others. Noah turned back, lost in his thoughts again, worried about the next move to be taken.

The green clouds over Mount Spuder were roaring and gathered all over, making it darker than ever. The spiders on Mount Spuder looked worried as if something unexpected was about to happen. They tried hiding in the cave and each possible hole they could find. The web all over was shaking as the wind blew them. And then something came flying with the speed of light, shattering the clouds. It was Googol who placed his feet on top of Mount Spuder, creating a quake. The spiders shivered at his arrival.

Googol settled, looked around, and smiled. "You all are so dirty."

Finding the web shattered on his entrance, spiders started coming out of their hideouts. They knew it was time to fight for their existence. The millions of spiders started gathering, each coming out from different ways. Some from holes, some from the top, some from beneath the stones. They knew the intruder was compelling and they had to work as a team to get him out. Googol was standing in between, looking in all directions to check the presence of the spiders, and then he smiled. "Really! Silly you are," Googol said calmly.

As Googol took his first step towards the cave of Crawler, one of the spiders jumped over him. Googol just waved his palm at that spider and she got converted to ash in the air. Googol again turned back and said, "Do you have an ashtray?"

As he turned back, the cadre of spiders attacked him to take over, but Googol could handle them all just with his hand. He stretched his hand and many of them turned to ashes. Some scared spiders started moving back while few of them still showed their faithfulness to Crawler and tried scratching Googol on his leg. "Why tickling me, baby?" Googol looked down and kicked the spiders crawling near him. As Googol walked straight assertively, the spiders walked along, keeping a safe distance and then gathered all over the entrance of the cave, cringing one over the other.

Googol reached the entrance of the cave of Crawler and then tried to look inside the dark side. Thousands of spiders immediately tried to cover up the entrance, creating a back to back wall and started webbing all over. Googol remained silent and watched them patiently, and once they finished blocking the access, Googol smiled and raised his hand to convert them all to ashes and unblocked his way. He then walked inside, placing his hands in his pocket. He pulled out a cigar and said 'Relume' to let the fire light the upper part of the cigar. "It's better now," Googol said and started walking inside digitigrade, as he wanted to avoid touching the dirt all over.

"Welcome, Googol," said Crawler in his heavy voice, sitting at the dead-end of the cave. Thousands of spiders were running and hiding behind Crawler and spreading all over his body. Hearing the sound, Googol stopped and raised the cigar to his face. He then saw the two black, round blinking eyes of Crawler. Googol tilted his head to have a look at the massive Crawler, and then said, "Crawler! It was my dream to meet you someday."

"Really?" Crawler replied sarcastically.

Googol smiled and took a step to the side and then continued, "I am not sure if your web is capable enough, so I came to inform to you that Dslots have entered the world of Electon."

"Saddest day for Electon," replied Crawler. As Crawler said this, the spiders started making noise which was loud and disturbing.

Googol pressed his ears and then said, "Can you ask your kids to be quiet when two wise men are talking?"

As Crawler looked to his sides, each of the spiders went silent. Googol then looked up again to continue, "I have come with an offer for you, Crawler."

"Oh! So someone who does not exist now is here to give an offer to the most powerful creature of Electon."

Googol now gave a sarcastic smile and then raised his hands to say in a strong and deep voice, "You are proud of your size, Crawler, not knowing the size of my brain. Time would come when the human race would believe my words more than anything else on this Earth. They would not only trust me but would be my followers. I will be God. I would be the name of the revolution in the change of their lifestyle. It would be me who would be standing with them for every small or big problem they would have. I would not only be on Earth but would extend my regime to galaxies. In the time of sorrow, in time of love, in time of respect, in time of fun, in time of laughter, it would be me who would carry all the humans along." Googol paused, and then with a husky voice said, coming near Crawler, "Humans would not even remember your name, Crawler."

Crawler was afraid if his words were correct, but he had seen the future and Crawler wanted to fight to not let it happen. Then Crawler said calmly, "They would be behind you, not knowing that you would be the reason for their grave."

Googol again smiled and then said with a pause, "You have two options, Crawler." He paused again and looked straight in the eyes of Crawler to continue, "Either join me and handover your warriors to me, else be ready to go to your grave."

As Googol stopped speaking, Crawler looked into his eyes. Crawler's eyes were gazing in anger and then he shouted vociferously, making a massive sound to even let Mount Spuder shake. The spiders started falling from the walls of the cave and Mount Spuder shook to make a loud noise. Crawler stood up as he had still been seated and started walking towards Googol in indignation. Googol took a step back, saying, "Do not make a mistake, Crawler. I am still not your present, you cannot hurt me. But yes, I can take away many lives here."

"This is the house of Spuder, Googol, and till my last breath, you will never be a part of the present. I existed because humans needed me but I never tried to become a need for humans. Remember, you exist because humans exist and if they vanish, you will be running from galaxy to galaxy."

Googol continued tramping as Crawler walked towards him, gnashed, and replied, "You still have time, Crawler. Think about my offer, else another option is always with my warriors."

Hearing him, Crawler again made a loud noise raising his front legs. His eyes grew wider and his long teeth became visible. He tried to hit Googol with his long, thorny legs, but Googol was all prepared with the clock of Venus to escape. As he vaporized, he shouted one last time, "The war is about to start, Crawler. Get ready."

The War Of Cigar Galaxy

About twelve million light-years away on planet Nebulous of the cigar galaxy, a fight was about to end which had lasted for decades. On Earth, this galaxy was discovered by Johann Elert Bode in the sixteenth century as being five times more luminous than the Milky Way and had its centre one hundred times more luminous than our galaxy's centre.

Nebulous was the planet at the centre of the cigar galaxy and was going through a war between Vslots and Dslots for ages. Nebulous was older than Earth and had seen what Earth was now exhibiting. The Electon world of Nebulous was on fire for a long time and Noah always wanted that to not be repeated on Earth.

Nebulous was the most beautiful planet of the cigar galaxy. For millions of years, it had green vegetation, water bodies, animals, and a microbe. The human race entered the planet late as compared to Earth. But they grew much faster and soon reached the stage of electromagnetic waves. Nebulous was highly energetic and had a high capability of solar masses. The Electon world of Nebulous was much more prosperous than what was on Earth. Vslots had an upper edge and never thought anything about Dslots. They never imagined that something like Dslots would ever come into existence and would create a grave for the planet. But it happened. Dslots entered the Electon world of the planet after the advancement of data in the mobile world of Nebulous.

Humans who were very active and energetic on Nebulous started getting lethargic and disconnected from their ancient values. People started spending more and more time on mobiles and lost personal touch and contact with friends and family. Vslots tried hard to stop the invasion but looked helpless at times. The mobile usage increased to the level that children stopped talking to their parents; sometime back, schools which were considered as the best time for children got shut down and children only studied on mobiles; gardens and play areas cause of being deserted were converted to mobile charging points so that children could sit and play mobile games live; love between people was left far behind; young boys and girls started marrying their mobile phones and chose them as their life partners; elders could only receive support and love from their children by visuals; energy sources from the planet were getting used for mobile devices; husbands and wives live chatted and emotional connection was given very low priority; people started only sitting and physical movement went to nil.

The result of extensive Dslots was that it slowly took away the aura of the humans from Nebulous. First, vegetation started to die on the planet as humans were not available to take care of them and use them as a source of energy for mobile devices; then animals got extinct as no one was available to take care of them and there was no vegetation left as food for them; and at last, humans started dying because of their own mistakes and carelessness.

The king of Vslot, named Supernove, was already killed and the war between Vslots and Dslots was at its last stage, so the death of the planet was on its verge.

The land of the Electon world of Nebulous was left with only dust and the blood of Vslots and Dslots after they had been engaged in the war for so long. Ooredo, captain of the Vslots, stood over a rock to examine the strength of the army of the Dslots. "We are not left with a choice," he paused as his leftover soldiers looked at him with hope, "but to fight for our existence."

His soldiers heard him and raised their digital swords to give a war cry, 'Rebelem'. Anuya, a keeper of spells of Vslots, took a step to reach next to Ooredo.

"Do we have a chance?"

Ooredo looked tensed and with a grave look replied, "Nebulous is dying, so are Vslots." He paused and then continued, "We tried our best but the human race of Nebulous chose death than life."

The wind blew, bringing the yellow dust along, and the sound of drums began from the other end by the army of Dslots. The war was again going to start after the long night. Ooredo looked up at the shining star, which could still be seen as the sun was yet to come up to spread its strength. The brightness of the sun of Nebulous was never so weak, but with time, the dust of ashes and death created a shield over it.

"You tried your best, Ooredo," said Anuya, with tears in her eyes.

The sound of drums increased. As a few outriders managed to squeeze through intact, the Vslot ground warriors stood up and raised their shields. The Vslot guards behind them levelled their ultraviolet spears over their comrades' shoulders.

"How many warriors are left with us, Anuya?" asked

Ooredo, still glued, looking at the massive army of the Dslots.

"Not more than ten thousand warriors, with the same number of children and young ladies," Anuya replied, looking at them and then added, "and they all are ready to fight for you after the death of King Supernove." Anuya took another step to reach closer to Ooredo and then said in a low voice, "We would be happy to die fighting for our Electon on Nebulous." Ooredo turned and looked into her eyes.

The dark green clouds were gathering above, covering the field to shield the most disastrous event on the planet. Ooredo knew that within a few hours or less, the entire race of Vslots from the planet Nebulous would be wiped off, and he would be lying somewhere getting scratched and burnt to death. The army of Dslots was a hundred times more then Vslots and they could not stand for long in front of them.

The drum beats grew stronger and through the fog in the war field, Ooredo could now see the array of Dslot soldiers walking towards them, heavily armed and with blood in their eyes. He looked despondent as he could not save his men and the existence of Vslots on Nebulous.

"What about Hydrazine craft?" Ooredo questioned, still focused on the army.

"Ready for your call."

"Sufficient for all? No one can be left," he said and then added, "not a single one."

Anuya nodded in confidence.

Ooredo looked at her and then said, "Let's leave." He turned, looked at his people to speak in a loud and clear voice, "We may have lost our Nebulous today, but we never lost hope. From thousands of years, Vslots have been fighting for their existence and it's time we join hands with different planets and different galaxies to save the human world, to save our Electon. If we live, we will be back and one fine day, our Nebulous will be called Vslot Nebulous." He paused and looked at his people who shouted and roared at his words and then continued, "Time to move to the Electon world of Earth; to return with full power and strength."

The people shouted and raised their swords to support him and created a loud voice. Everyone, including Ooredo and Anuya, looked up as three huge Hydrazine crafts arrived in the sky.

The Hydrazine craft was the space shuttle of Vslot made up of dark black tectonic plate rocks of the planet Nebulous and run using Hydrazine fuel, which is a colourless volatile alkaline liquid with powerful reducing properties, used in chemical synthesis.

As the craft reached closer to the ground, the wind started blowing, letting the dust create a fog cloud. "Rush fast to board the craft," shouted Ooredo and started helping his people to board the craft. Anuya took care of children and young ones, helping them to board the ship. The Dslot, at the far end, observed the entry of the craft and knew Vslots would be evacuating the planet. Some of the Dslots started celebrating while others began running towards them so that they can kill maximum number of Vslots before they leave the planet. Ooredo time to time turned back to check the movement of Dslots and motivated his people to be quick.

Once Ooredo ensured that each one of his people was on the ship, he stepped back on the rock, followed by Anuya, looked at the Dslots still approaching, and said, "A time will come when they will be running."

Anuya went on her knees and bowed the ground to

say, "Sorry, my Nebulous, for leaving you alone but some decisions are taken to bring changes in the universe."

They finally boarded the craft before Dslots could approach them. "Let's take the path to Earth, Milky Way galaxy."

The Hydrazine craft started rising from the ground, leaving a storm of dust and stones and vanished with the speed of electromagnetic waves.

Remembering Milla

After losing the task, Roger was sad, and so he decided to visit the human world. After entering Electon, he understood his real motto in life but he was not able to forget the human world which safeguarded him for years. Maybe his attachment to the human world is what made him more concerned about humans and save them from Dslots in the future. Roger took permission from Emma to visit the human world and so he approached the Alva room. He pushed the door and walked towards the Alva bulb. He looked at it with a grave look as he still missed Milla and wanted to meet her grandmother, who was left all alone. He knew Milla betrayed him but he was concerned about her ninety-nine-year-old grandmother.

"Avalonia," Roger said, looking at the Alva bulb, and his body started to evaporate to enter the bulb. Within no time, he was standing in front of the house of Milla. He looked puzzled and sad looking at the place where he had spent some enjoyable times with her.

"I miss you, Milla," Rhythm said with tears in his eyes.

He then walked to ring the bell.

"Wait, I am old and may take some time to open,"

he heard the voice of her grandmother from inside.

The door opened after some time and Milla's grandmother stood in front of him, taking the support of her stick, wearing a white flower printed gown. She adjusted her spectacles and then smiled, saying, "Oh! Rhythm, pleasure to have you at my place."

"I was wondering about you as I did not meet you since days, grandma," Rhythm said, taking hold of her hand, and they both walked inside.

"Milla is still in Aachen. What to say about this girl, she didn't even bother to call me over the landline." She paused and then continued offering the seat to Rhythm, "Did she contact you, Rhythm?"

"No, not yet, grandma. She will be fine," Rhythm replied, taking a seat over the blue sofa placed at the corner.

She too took a seat, placing her stick to the side, and then said, "Times have changed a lot. Everyone is busy with their own stuff, who cares about the old lady."

"Why do you say this? Look, I care for you and I am always here for you," Rhythm said, looking at her and was concerned for her as she was left all alone.

Grandmother smiled and then said, "I baked a cake for Christmas, would you like to taste it? You can tell me if Milla would like it too."

Rhythm was sad on hearing this as he knew Milla was never going to return, but he still never let it reflect on his face, and replied, "Sure, grandma. You may tell me, I'll get it from the kitchen."

"So nice of you. It's placed on the left side on the upper shelf," she directed him as Rhythm stood up from his seat to enter the kitchen, which was behind her.

Rhythm reached the kitchen and started looking at the shelves and when he saw a chocolate cake placed in a glass bowl on the top, he said, "Yes, I got it."

"Good, you must bring a spoon and a plate as well. They are placed on the lower side of the kitchen shelves, Roger," she added.

"Okay, grandmother," said Rhythm, and then he stopped astound. He realized that grandmother called him Roger. How would she know his name from the Electon world? He then looked at the cake which was on the upper shelve. How could she place the cake on the top shelf as she had a bent back?

He moved to the kitchen door slowly and found Milla's grandmother standing straight in front of him without her stick, smiling, "The game is not over yet, Roger."

CHALYAARA.COM™

Ghoomna to Banta Hai!

Enjoy 20% Discounted Trip To Bangkok- Pattaya, offered by our Travel Partner Chalyaara.com.

How to get the offer?

1. Fill Up the form below:

Full Name	
Age	
City	
E-mail Id	
Mobile Number	
Review about Book	
Number of people to travel	

2. Click a Family Selfy, along with the Book "Rhythm Roger"
3. Send (WhatsApp) a picture of this page and the Selfy on below number: 8803388803 (Chalyaara.com Number) and 8810329026 (Authors Number)
4. Chalyaara.com team will call you to plan your travel and provide you the offer mentioned above.

Terms and Conditions:

1. This voucher is not redeemable for cash.
2. There will be no replacements provided if this voucher is lost, stolen, destroyed or used without permission.
3. Winner needs to inform us at least 45 days before his travel plan.
4. Discount will be provided on actual tariff, not on the discounted fare.
5. This voucher is not valid during peak season, festival & long weekends.
6. Only the winner can redeem this voucher. (Not any relative, family member, etc., the winner must be a part of the trip).
7. The offer is valid on the complete package (excluding Flight).

☐ I agree with the above terms and condition and is interested in taking the above offer.

Signature: